Wounded Sparks

Nicolas Remington

Contents

Prologue

I suppose this is how men feel sometimes, I thought to myself, when absolutely random women show up on their doorsteps and claim to be their baby mamas.

Except that this was vice versa.

Angelo Donafrio was looking at me expectantly, waiting for any sign of a response to his incredible revelation. It was strange to feel so claustrophobic in my airy living room. It was strange to feel the beginnings of a hot sweat when the wind was billowing furiously outside and rainclouds were gathering. But it was even stranger to feel nothing – no zing of attraction to his shifty green eyes and bulging biceps – for the man who'd wanked into a cup for cash and donated it to a loser of a woman like me.

I vaguely remembered a picture of a caramel-skinned man with jet-black hair and the greenest eyes I'd ever seen. Granted, it was all a tiny bit cloudy in my imagination after three years but as soon as I'd seen that photo, I'd decided That's him. That's the man I want. Not want sexually. I was very clear about that with my conscience. For starters, he was nameless – just a gorgeous face with a healthy family history and good genes. He was an image of what my child could look like in the distant future. Besides that, he would never know who I was, either. Confidentiality, that's what the sperm bank had emphatically promised.

Yet here he was, sitting across me in my living room with an untouched mug of black coffee and a plate of shortbread before him.

Realising that I wasn't going to say anything anytime soon, Angelo said gently, "I know this is a little hard for you to –"

"How did you get my address?" I interjected, sounding angrier than I'd intended. *And what the hell happened to you?*

Sure, I hadn't seen a picture of his entire body but body ink and piercings weren't high on my list of attractive aspects of a person and I had made that clear at the bank as well. I had been extremely picky when it came to whose sperm I wanted inside me and a tattooed miscreant certainly hadn't been what I'd wanted. Still, my son was healthy and that was what counted.

Healthy is a relative term, though, said a sad voice in my head. I shook it away.

"Don't worry about that," said Angelo, his eyes boring into mine. His last name sounded familiar and I couldn't think why. I didn't want to think why. "I don't wanna take him from you, cupcake. You can believe that. Hell, I don't even like kids."

I got to my feet. "Then what do you want?"

"To see him. Just to see him."

"No," I said. "Get out."

"Excuse me?" He stood up slowly, his steady smile disappearing from his face.

My pistol's upstairs, I thought, my eyes straying skyward. But he'd probably get to me before I could get there.

"You're thinking about how fast you can get your gun, right?" He chuckled at my shocked expression. "Females get all shifty-eyed when they think they're in danger," he explained, a cheeky grin on his face. "It wasn't exactly rocket science to guess that you'd be packing something."

"I should never have let you in," I said to myself. Louder and with a rage I knew I had to keep in check, I snarled, "I'm going to sue everybody. Starting with that half-arsed clinic! And then you."

He smiled as if I'd just told him I liked fast cars. "That kid of yours has my blood in his veins. I have a right to see him."

"You have no rights!" I spluttered with dismay. "That was the whole bloody point of getting inseminated! That I wouldn't have to deal with male bullshít like this! He's my son – not yours."

"Yeah? What'll happen when he asks about his daddy?" Unlike mine, his voice was low and controlled. "Will you tell him how you picked the donor out of a catalogue like an armchair? I'm offering you a lifeline here, baby."

I bit my bottom lip, the severity of his questions hitting me like a hurricane. Of course I'd spent sleepless nights wondering what I'd tell my son about his father when he'd inevitably ask. Freak accident? Deadbeat? One-night stand? What would sound believable? What would be appropriate to tell a child?

"That's none of your concern. Just leave."

"You know I'm right, Danielle. The poor kid's gonna –"

My front door was rammed open before he could even finish his sentence. I let out a scream and jumped, knocking the table in the process and sending the scalding coffee onto Angelo's bare legs. He hissed out a curse, falling back onto the couch and grimacing in pain.

"Where is he?" someone was yelling, threatening to wake my son up in the process. "Angelo, you imbecilic pus! Where are you?"

"Shít," Angelo murmured under his breath.

"Don't come into my house and bellow like this!" I screamed back at the disembodied voice, heading into the passageway to intercept whoever it was who could refer to someone as 'imbecilic pus'. Mickey was still fast asleep and I wanted to keep it that way. "Who the hell are you?" I asked, although I had a vague idea.

Sure, he was taller than Angelo by a good three inches but the resemblance was uncanny. The only real difference was that instead of a wife-beater-and-shorts ensemble, this particular male specimen favoured a black suit and a scowl.

"Carlo Donafrio," he said forebodingly, his voice tinged with a hint of an Italian accent. "Where the hell is Angie?"

"Come on in, cuz," Angelo said from behind me, and I spun around to glare at him, still reeling from his 'cuz's' utter rudeness.

"What is this, a family reunion?" I spat.

Carlo boorishly pushed past me, squaring off his cousin. "How could you do this to me, you dipshit? Do you have any idea what –"

"Easy, man. I was just curious. We all were."

"So you hacked into those files to sate your curiosity?" Carlo barked, and a cry from upstairs punctuated his question.

"Now look what you've done," I grumbled, shoving past the pair of them and bounding upstairs.

Mickey's cries had picked up momentum and by the time I'd scooped his heavy form up and pressed him against my chest, he was wordlessly letting me know that he had no intention of shutting up anytime soon.

Carlo Donafrio.

So familiar.

And then, like a lightning bolt, it finally hit me. His photos were usually splashed in the Daily Herald under headlines like 'Alleged Murderer Acquitted' or 'Italian Billionaire Crime Lord Pleads Not Guilty to Drug Syndicate Scandal'. He wore Armani religiously, as Jules, my best friend, was always quick to point out. He had six yachts docked all over the world. His passport could get full in only a month. He was the world's most dangerous thirty-year-old. Jude loved the tabloids and soaked up everything like it was the gospel.

And he's downstairs arguing with the man that wanked into a cup to help me make Mickey, I thought with a shudder. Dear God. What are the odds?

"Ssh, my baby," I said gently, slamming the door shut and locking it. Inside, I was hyperventilating.

My mobile was downstairs, nestled somewhere in the couch I'd been sitting on. I had yet to invest in a telephone upstairs and now that would be my downfall.

Dear God, please don't let them hurt my baby.

Perhaps Carlo Donafrio was into selling babies on the black market and used his cousin – if they were indeed related, which I strongly suspected they were – as a worm to infiltrate the homes of stupidly trusting single mothers like me.

Mickey was screaming blue murder and, awkwardly manoeuvring him in my arms, I offered him a heavy breast as a peace offering. Latching onto it, he began to vigorously suck while I made soft cooing sounds. There were so many things I felt for this boy and protective was top of the list. He was three and could hardly walk or speak. I still breastfed him. To me – someone who'd never thought she'd have a child – he was perfect. Nothing was wrong with him.

"No one will ever hurt you, sweetheart," I promised him, my voice fierce. As if he understood my intensity, his eyes widened as he continued to suckle my nipple.

And then the doorknob was turned and I instantly shut up, my heart hammering my chest.

"Ms. Clarke?"

"What?" My voice was little more than a croak. I didn't want that, didn't want that feebleness. Clearing my throat, I said more assertively, "What the hell do you want?"

Sated, Mickey released my nipple and replaced it with a tiny thumb. It was his face I was thinking about when the door was kicked open, hanging off its latches. Shrieking, I jumped back, nearly stumbling over a stray toy.

Carlo Donafrio stood in the doorway, his eyes blazing. "Let me see the boy," he said sharply, as if kicking doors in were a natural occurrence.

"You must be out of your mind," I hissed, quickly snapping my top over my chest.

"What did Angelo tell you?"

"Get out, you...you drug lord! And...and don't kill me," I added as an afterthought. I held Mickey tightly in my arms. He was squirming slightly, my grip on him obviously too stifling.

Carlo paused mid-step and raised a speculative brow. "Am I to take it that you believe everything you read in the papers?" He waited for a response and received none. "Perhaps you believe that I am going to gouge your eyes out and shove them down your throat with a baby in your arms? Or, even better, sell the both of you on the black market?"

I reddened, because the idea of baby trafficking had crossed my mind. It felt realer when he himself said it aloud.

"You don't have to be afraid of me," he continued. "I promise you, this is the last time you'll see me. My cousin will be dealt with for imposing, I can assure you."

Breathe, Dani. Just breathe, I told myself, glancing at Mickey, who was looking up at me with inquiring green eyes. He'd been born with the most dazzling sky-blue eyes, but as soon as he'd hit six months or so, they'd darkened to the pale emerald they were now. Angelo's had been dark and playful.

"Where is he? Your cousin, I mean," I said softly, unwillingly meeting Carlo's eyes.

"Why? Do you find him attractive?"

"Excuse me?" I nearly shouted, disturbed by the notion he'd think I was interested in that...person.

"Don't worry about it." He crossed the room in two strides and loomed over me, his presence like a thick cloud.

I had the fierce urge to cower and hide my son from him, as if he were the devil coming to collect firstborn sons. Instead, I stood my ground, clutching Mickey to me. It was fascinating to watch Carlo watch him. He stared down at my son for what seemed like ages but could've only been seconds, before he lifted his head and met my gaze.

"He is mine," he declared in a low voice.

I took an uneasy step back. "No...but Angelo is –"

"Angelo is nothing!" He exhaled sharply when he noticed my obvious fear. "I think you should sit down for this one." He shot me a look that told me he meant it. "After all, I wouldn't want anything to happen to my son."

Chapter 1

"You have to go to the police, Dani," said Adam.

"But after we beat the accent out of him," Charlie added menacingly, giving me the look he saved for his special I'm-your-twin-so-you-best-listen-to-me moments.

I was sitting at our father's chipped wooden kitchen table, a cup of black coffee warming my hands and an untouched slice of Marmite-slathered toast before me. I needed the coffee more than my brothers could ever know. It took everything in my power to keep from succumbing to sleep and dreaming about my Mickey growing up and becoming a bloody talented drug dealer.

God forbid, I thought morosely, gingerly taking another sip of the coffee.

"Well?" Adam pressed, folding his arms across his chest as he moved to stand in front of the sink beside his younger brother. In a frayed, grey Crowing Uni rugby T-shirt and black shorts decorated with tiny Tweety and Sylvester images, he hardly looked like a dangerous character. Carlo Donafrio would pummel him to a pulp before he could even lift an arm to swing a punch.

"I'm not going to the police and you're not beating the...the accent out of Donafrio," I said slowly.

Charlie visibly deflated. "Why not?"

"Because," I said, remembering Carlo's curt explanation of what had transpired three years ago, "he promised to never come near me or Mickey again."

Adam, who was two years older than Charlie and me, rolled his eyes. "Right – and the word of a known crook should be taken as the gospel."

"The fact that you can't even sue that fúcking joke of a clinic –" Charlie began, but I cut him off.

"Can we please not talk about this?" I said, letting out an exasperated sigh. "And don't tell Dad. Or Mum. About anything."

"Don't tell Dad what?" My father's voice came from behind me as he sauntered into the room, the morning paper in hand. "Morning, sweetheart," he said, pecking the top of my head. He didn't sound especially startled to find all three of his grown-up children in his kitchen on a balmy Saturday morning. Adam and Charlie practically still lived at home with him. "When did you get here?" he added, pulling open the refrigerator.

Did I really want to explain to him that I'd crept in last night with Mickey fast asleep in my arms? That I felt safer in my old bedroom? That I wanted my brothers around me because they were free security?

"Just a little while ago," I lied, daring my brothers to say otherwise. They didn't.

"Where's my grandson?"

"Upstairs."

"Everything all right?" Dad was looking at me, a glass of orange juice in hand. His rheumy blue eyes seemed to be searching mine. It wasn't fair that my father could tell when I was lying just by glancing at me.

"Dad, got a minute?" said Adam, springing into action. "It's about my Merc."

Just like that, I lost our father's attention. His eyes swivelled to my big brother, excitement emanating from his tall form. Car talk was the closest thing to Disneyland for Dad. Top Gear was like a child's cartoon to him, so it was no wonder that he instantly launched into a heated interrogation about Adam's Mercedes SLK with gusto. That gave me enough time to slink out of the kitchen – except that Charlie followed me upstairs.

"How a guy like that was allowed to sell his jizz, I'll never know," he said in a low voice so our father wouldn't hear. My parents were under the impression that Mickey was the product of a one-night stand. "What's next? Slenderman adopting?"

I rolled my eyes. "That's a fictional character. And I'd rather not talk about this, thank you very much."

"You need to talk about this, Dani. This guy barged into your house. This guy wants something and if you're too dense to see it, I'll say it for you."

Charlie was cute when he pretended he was older. Sometimes, I believed it, especially now, when I stared at his intense baby blues and the stubborn jut of his jaw. He was almost a foot taller than me despite being a runt as a child. Being fraternal twins, most people had simply assumed that I was older than him by a few years.

"What do you think he wants?" I asked, genuinely curious. Charlie's mind worked differently to other people, which might've been the result of multiple head trauma on his motorcycle. As a child, he hadn't believed the stork-and-baby story our father had half-heartedly told us. Instead, he'd conjured up the notion that women swallowed baby seeds and the end result was a baby to call their own.

"Isn't it obvious?" said Charlie, glancing at the mahogany cot he'd built with Adam. Mickey was stirring inside. "Don't you watch mob movies? He wants an heir."

"You're being ridiculous," I said, scooping up my son and burying my face in his mop of thick, dark curls.

"Think about it." He began to pace my bedroom. "He shows up out of nowhere and suddenly wants to see if someone bought his cream and if said person had a son, right? Well, either he's dying of a fatal disease and wants an heir to continue his legacy of crime and mayhem, or his gran's on his case."

"If you must know, it was all a misunderstanding," I said sharply.

"What do you mean?"

I took a deep breath. "Three years ago, he wasn't much of a bad guy. He wasn't bad." I met Charlie's disbelieving stare. "Anyway, his sister-in-law – who'd lost her husband, by the way – wanted a child so badly. She told Carlo that he was the next best thing to her late husband, so after she battled to persuade him, he finally –"

"Is there a point to this story, or do you enjoy romanticising this man?"

I shot him a dirty look. "He finally visited the sperm bank and everything was going okay until she changed her mind and said it would be like dishonouring his brother." I set Mickey back in his cot and he promptly grabbed a rattle in his fat hands. "Instead of discarding his sperm, the clinic just...kept it. And then I came along and his picture was there and...well, here's Mickey."

"You're kidding me." Charlie ran a hand through his dirt-blonde hair. "Danielle," he said, using my full name, "you have to stay away from him, mistake or no. The guy's dangerous."

"I know that."

"Do you?" Adam appeared in the doorway. "You've always done whatever the hell you please, Danielle, and most of your decisions are a joke."

"What are you trying to say?" I said through clenched teeth, folding my arms across my chest.

They stood together, towering over me. "That you're so small and this world is so big."

"And now you're both ganging up on me. Thank you," I muttered.

They were both utterly wrong. Carlo Donafrio wasn't going to come near someone like me. Besides, I wouldn't let him.

At twenty-eight, I certainly should've been considering settling down, but after witnessing what had happened between my parents, that was reason enough to stay away from wedding aisles and tulle gowns and anything to do with what was a different kind of life sentence.

It was this thought that sprang to mind when Charlie's ex-girlfriend – my somewhat best friend – Libby Wilson showed up at my café and asked me to be her maid-of-honour.

"I know things have been awkward between us after Charlie and I broke up but really, Dee, it would mean the world to me if you'd agree," she said over the din in the café, absently picking up a chocolate-glazed slice of cake that was on display on the counter and dipping a finger in the icing.

"Awkward?" I said sarcastically. "You only dumped him on his birthday. Nothing awkward about that."

Libby sighed, putting her finger to her mouth. "Oh yes, because Charlie's been so heartbroken. In fact, so heartbroken that he's had a string of girlfriends since."

"That's Charlie we're talking about," I said, smiling despite myself. "He doesn't know the meaning of the word." However, I did know my brother well enough to know that his sleeping around was his way of coping with being dumped by the love of his life – not that he'd ever say that aloud.

Libby gave me a wry smile, her eyes dancing. "So I take it that's a yes? You'll show up at that lovely boutique on Stone this weekend? I'm thinking violet gowns."

I nodded. "Do you have a cake?"

She giggled. "I've got two months to decide that...but I'd like you to design it. Sponge."

"Naturally," I told her. And she sauntered out, the bell clinging to note her exit.

I breathed a sigh of relief after she'd left. Libby and I weren't exactly estranged but we rarely saw each other, despite pretending to be sisters since pre-school, pigtails and Play-Doh. Of course, I knew that Charlie had something to do with it. Out of solidarity, I was sticking by him.

Oh well.

If Lib thought a shotgun marriage with a guy named Zed was what she needed, who was I to hold that against her?

"Dani?" Megan popped up beside me and I turned my attention to her. "I just got a call..."

"What is it?" I snapped. Megan had the annoying habit of dragging things out.

"You know your pastiera? I just got a huge order for it."

"Well, that's great news," I exclaimed, all the while wondering how huge she meant when she said 'huge'. Pastiera tasted better when it was made days before consumption. "Just let me know who, when and where."

Megan swallowed. "Mia Donafrio's having a birthday party next weekend."

Mia Donafrio.

How was it that in the short space of roughly two weeks, 'Donafrio' was becoming a household name? Was there no end to my misfortune? Was it a coincidence that Carlo's sister-in-law just happened to order a traditional Italian cake that could've been made by the many traditional Italian pastry shops in my vicinity?

No.

There was no such thing as a coincidence.

This sentiment was emphasised by the sound of the door dinging as it was pushed open, and Carlo Donafrio himself stepped inside. Megan gave me a sideways glance, and I knew exactly what she was thinking.

Is he going to hold us at gunpoint?

She didn't have to say it aloud.

"May I help you?" I said as professionally as I could, ignoring the sudden lull in conversation at the few occupied tables at the front.

It didn't help that Donafrio looked like he had murder in his eyes, or that he'd appeared in the paper over the weekend and was accused of the kidnapping and torture of an Irish club owner, or that a man who had 'BODYGUARD' stamped across his forehead was standing at the door as conspicuous as a tsunami.

Or all of the above.

Either way, I wasn't about to be intimidated, especially under his un-blinking stare. "May I help you?" I repeated, and Megan slithered away.

"Clarke's," he intoned, finally taking his eyes off me and surveying my coffee shop. "Very quaint."

By 'quaint', he probably meant the red-and-white checked colour scheme. Someone had once said that it made the café seem like a little piece of 'gran's kitchen'. I took that as a compliment.

"Have you come here as a health inspector?" I couldn't help my sarcastic tone.

"Not at all," he replied seriously. "I require a slice of your pastiera napo-letana. I'm told that it's the real deal."

"Why me?" I blurted out. I was mortified when a blush enflamed my cheeks when he gave me a slow smile. I was positive that he usually beamed like that when he considered how many ways he could kill a person.

"Because you are the best, cara. Do you doubt that your skills are no match for a Neapolitan's tastebuds?"

"I didn't know you were from Naples." And why should you, Dani? The less you know about this man, the better. "Not that I care. I mean, I have work to do. One slice of cake?"

He nodded. "And I would like to talk to you."

"About?" I snapped.

"About the boy."

Charlie's words reverberated in my ear: He wants an heir.

But that was silly, wasn't it? Perhaps he was going to sue the fertility clinic for not discarding his deposit. Perhaps he simply needed to inform me. Why not over a slice of cake I'd slaved to make?

"He has a name," I found myself saying. "I don't appreciate your referring to him as if he's an arbitrary creature."

"Mickey," he said, his bottom lip curling in distaste. "Are you a fan of the mouse?"

I didn't know if he was being sarcastic or serious, so I replied through clenched teeth, "It's short for Michael, after my father. Not that that's any of your business."

"Au contraire, Danielle Clarke. It is my business," he snarled, making me take a step back.

No, I thought. You will not take my baby away from me! You have no right to!

"But...but you said –"

"What I said and what I am saying have no relation. Live in the present. There are matters we must discuss." With that, he turned on his heel and claimed an empty table by the windows. He looked completely out of place in his suit and the square table was dwarfed by his size. Mumbling to myself, I went to the glass chest of cakes and cut a large slice of pastiera and set it on a plate, bringing it to Carlo myself.

I reluctantly took the seat opposite him, instantly regretting my choice of purchasing cute, dinky tables. Our legs instantly brushed under the table and, as discreetly as I could, I pulled back and all but squished them under my chair.

"Grazie," he said quietly.

"What is it?" I muttered, settling my eyes somewhere past his shoulder.

"Look at me when I'm speaking to you."

I did, glaring at him. "I wasn't aware that I was back in primary school, Headmaster."

"When you behave half your age, Ms. Clarke, control is warranted." He dug his fork into the cake. As if in a trance, I watched him put it to his mouth. His lips were full, a faint pink; rough stubble dusting the skin above his top lip and the jut of his jaw.

I bet those lips are just as dangerous as the man that uses them.

Horrified, I looked away.

"Delizioso," Carlo murmured, putting the fork down. His eyes had closed. "My nonna would make this every Easter. The ricotta she used was the most delectable." His eyes flew open again. "This comes very close to my grandmother's."

I leaned forward. "Is she still alive?"

A cloud passed over his face. "No, but she lived to be ninety-seven." The poker face returned. "Wouldn't you call that amazing?"

"She certainly honoured her parents," I mused, remembering how my grandmother had told my brothers and me as children to 'honour thy parents so you may live a long and happy life'. She'd passed away the year after, still so young. Charlie's response to the news was: "She must've been a nightmare to our great-grandparents."

"Are you religious?" Carlo questioned, taking another forkful of cake.

"I believe in God," I replied guardedly. "Are you?"

"I have yet to see the point of religion." His eyes met mine.

If someone had told me that I would find myself discussing religion with Carlo Donafrio, suspected killer-slash-mobster-slash-drug dealer and definite billionaire, in my coffee shop with our knees touching, I would've laughed in that person's face and suggested a mental facility to them.

Yet here we were.

"I...I have to...check the stock," I said gently, unable to tear my eyes from his.

"Ms. Clarke, it would be greatly appreciated if you could bring...Michael to my office whenever you are free, preferably this week." This was his idea of cutting to the chase.

"To your office?" I hissed. "Have you completely lost the plot? Why would I do that?"

It was Carlo's turn to lean forward. "Because I know where you live," he intoned in a low voice.

A shiver crawled down my spine. "Why are you doing this?"

"We are both the victims of the Healey Group's incompetence," he said gruffly. "My lawyers are in the process of issuing summons. Please – don't look like a rabbit in the headlights – you won't have to appear in court, unless it is absolutely necessary. I'm not the type to get taken for a ride, Ms. Clarke."

I swallowed. "And how will you explain finding me in the first place? That your cousin simply happened to stumble upon confidential information?"

"If I had known that helping a family member out would have resulted in such a ridiculous mistake, I would never have even considered it." His voice was like shards of glass. "You must understand where I'm coming from."

"My son," I spat, "is not a mistake. You are the mistake. Men like you should be neutered." I was used to people thinking awful things about my son, a three-year-old who could barely walk, barely string two words together. Pitying me. Pitying him. Mistake.

Carlo's eyes became slits. "Don't insult my intelligence with childish jibes."

"How dare you call my son a mistake? I didn't ask for your sperm to be put inside me!"

The silence that followed made the hair stand on my neck. I turned in my seat to find every eye in the room on us. I was done being embarrassed.

"What?" I yelled. "Why don't you lot drink your fúcking tea and mind your own business?" I turned back to face the man before me, a scowl on my face. "What?" He had the semblance of a leer on his face.

"Something you said," he murmured. "You must have seen something you liked in my picture, cara, so in essence, you wanted me."

My mouth went dry, even as I felt the flutter in my belly. "Leave. Leave and never come back."

"Certainly." He got to his feet, his cologne moving with the air. "Now I can tell Mia that I have tasted a piece of Naples. I'm sure twenty cakes won't be a problem for a woman as talented as you, Ms. Clarke."

I watched him leave, relief sinking in. It was only when his black BMW sped away that I realised that he hadn't paid for his cake – and what did I expect from a crook?

Chapter 2

"You look like sleep is a ghost and you've been chasing it," Mum informed me, setting a cup of green tea on the table before me. "This is Jazz's remedy for insomnia."

I hated green tea and my mother knew it, so why she was trying to get me to chug down her girlfriend's stupid, so-called remedy was beyond me. As tactfully as I could, I pushed the cup away and sighed, suddenly feeling claustrophobic in Mum's immense kitchen.

"Mickey's keeping me up at night," I lied, when truthfully, it was the possibility of serving him up to the criminal that helped make him that was giving me sleepless nights.

My mother's eyes glittered with love for her grandson. "You know you can leave him here whenever you want, pet. He loves his gran."

"Of course," I said. "But Jazz loves her sleep."

"Don't be like that." My mother instantly closed up and busied herself at the sink.

It was like "that" whenever I made it plain that I despised Jasmine Lewis' very existence. If it wasn't for her, my parents would probably still be together and I wouldn't have had to come home from school one day and discover that my mother's gay and my parents were splitting up. Adam and Charlie were absolutely cool with it. Having a lesbian mother gave them some sort of weird street cred. They'd never come home with tears in their eyes because their friends had suddenly turned on them and called their mother a carpet-muncher and other filthy names. Naturally, their friends found it quite hot.

"Do you ever think of Dad?" I turned in my seat to get a better look at her.

"Michael and I are quite good friends." She didn't bother to fix her eyes on me.

"Would you ever go back to him?"

This time, she spun around, her brow furrowed. "Danielle, you're a big girl now. You're not a child; you're an adult. You know how relationships are. How can I go back to your father when I love Jazz?"

As if on cue, Jazz herself sauntered into the kitchen, the scent of sweet oils filling the air. Her waist-length salt-and-pepper hair was done into a neat French braid that snaked down her spine, a crown of daisies on her head. In a purple gypsy top and flowing, white ankle-length skirt to finish whatever look she was going for, she was still as OTT as I'd thought she was all those years ago when she'd introduced herself as Mum's "friend".

"Danielle!" she said, clapping her hands together when she saw me at their table. "I had no idea you were here."

I hated everything about her – from her wacky dress sense to her lilting I'm-more-posh-than-you accent. Everything. I was still coming to terms with my mother's poor taste in lovers.

"I was just leaving," I said, sniffing as I got to my feet.

"Where's Michael?" she asked, bending down to peck my mother's cheek. That was another thing about Jasmine Lewis – she was a giantess standing at six-foot-something while my mum was a dwarf in comparison. It was unnerving to say the least.

"He's with a friend of mine," I offered vaguely. I knew I was being immature but I couldn't help it whenever I was in the same room as Goliath the Home-Wrecker. "Have a lovely day, Mum."

"But you've only been in for half an hour, Dani," she protested.

"Yes, well, Jules can't take care of Mickey the entire morning," I muttered, and left the kitchen, heading out the front door.

Once inside my car, I could see them both peeking out the kitchen window at me.

Magic Mike was on the television, a half-empty bottle of red was on my coffee table, and my son was fast asleep upstairs after being in a massive strop and getting his dinner all over me. I was an awful mother for drinking when I was supposed to be breastfeeding.

All in all, I supposed it was a great way to end a perfectly dreary Saturday. Jules, my best friend, had gone clubbing and since both Adam and Charlie had dates, there was no one to babysit Mickey. Dad was out of commission after experiencing the mother of all hangovers Friday evening and never really getting out of bed. Mum and Jazz were completely out of the question.

Good wine and gyrating men onscreen would have to do it.

Because this is what my life has come to, I thought with the dull ache that usually came with yet another weekend spent alone.

It wasn't that I didn't date. It was just that I didn't see the point when they were just going to leave me. It didn't matter how amazing the first few weeks were; I was absolutely paranoid about being dumped. Therapists would probably say that I put myself in my father's shoes; that I didn't want to end up like him – alone in a house full of memories with nothing but Top Gear and my grown sons to console me.

I'd never really asked him about the divorce. I figured it was much too painful for him to even think about. My mother had been the love of his life. That's what he'd said in his vows. He'd been through enough humiliation. When my mother had come out, she hadn't exactly been quiet about it. All their friends had gotten a letter in the post explaining "the change in her life".

She hadn't stopped to think about my life. Perhaps I was being utterly selfish and childish but what she'd done hadn't just affected Dad.

I took another swig of wine from my glass, the picture on the screen becoming a bit blurry.

"I think that's enough," a voice said from behind me, somewhere over the couch.

I squeezed my eyes shut and opened them again.

"No, you're not hallucinating," Carlo confirmed, reaching down and snatching the glass from me. He came around my couch and set it on the table. "Is this what you do in your free time?" he wanted to know, his lip curling with disgust.

"How the hell did you get in?" I looked him over. The man probably slept in Armani suits.

"You need to invest in proper locks," he told me, picking up the wine bottle and examining the label. "And you need better taste."

"Who died and made you my student counsellor?" Wobbling, I heaved myself off the couch. "Please get out."

"Where's Michael?"

"No. Look, should I say this in Italian?" I cleared my throat. "Vat..."

"Vattene?" he said helpfully.

"Yes. That."

"No. We need to talk about your complete refusal to do what I asked."

"You might be used to bullying and coercion to get what you want but I'm not –"

His hand moved to my mouth, silencing me. "Ssh. Do you hear that?"

What I did hear was the sound of blood rushing to my head at his touch. What I did hear was my heartbeat speeding up to Olympic-marathon proportions. What I didn't hear – until Carlo pointed it out – was my son's explosion of cries.

Before I could stop him, Carlo was heading upstairs, taking the stairs two at a time. I stumbled behind him, gripping the banister for support and cursing my low alcohol tolerance. By the time I staggered into the nursery, Carlo had already scooped Mickey up, barely breaking a sweat. My son's cries had died down to more of a sorrowful whimper.

"That's good, mio figlio. Crying is for babies," he was saying in a low voice. "You are three. A big boy."

"He is a baby," I put in, though he really wasn't.

Carlo's mouth became a thin line. "What if I had not been here? Would you have tripped in here to pick him up? Cristo santo!Is this what you do on a regular basis?"

"Oh God, would you shut up?" I screamed. "What do you want from me? To take my son away? To make my life a living hell? Do you really want someone to take over your coke-smuggling business? To become a...a cruel monster and thug like you?"

"What are you talking about, Danielle?"

I couldn't get the image of Mickey in his arms out of my mind now even if I tried. Mickey rarely took to new people – he was difficult like that – and the fact that he was now quietly sucking on his index finger in Carlo's arms said a lot.

"I don't want you to corrupt my child," I said softly, sobering up in that second. "I won't have him turn into...into you. So I think it's best if you never see us again."

Carlo placed a gentle kiss on Mickey's mop of hair before returning him to his cot. Straightening up, he turned to fix his piercing green eyes on me. "You think it's best if I never see you again," he repeated, approaching me with the look a lion gives its prey. "Do you really think you can tell me what to do?"

I reached out and moved his suit jacket aside, exposing his waist. As I'd expected, a gun was sitting comfortably in its holster.

"A Glock. Cute," I muttered, retracting my hand. I looked him in the eye. "I think this says everything, don't you?"

"Protection."

"Danger," I countered, and he scowled at me.

"Do you know how many people are out to get me, cara? Too many to even count."

"Exactly. They're out to get you – not Mickey. But if you keep creeping around here, you'll be putting him at risk," I said through clenched teeth. "I won't have that."

"I would never let anything happen to him."

"You're not God. You can't control everything."

Silence stretched for an interminable moment before he said in a low voice, "Just remember Mia's birthday party next weekend. You have all the details."

"Sure."

"Sleep well," he said.

"You, too."

"I don't sleep."

"Just put them in the kitchen," Mia barked, leading the way into her house.

Megan gave me a sideways glance, her hands quaking.

"Careful," I hissed at her. "You'll drop the cake."

"I can't help it," she whispered back. "These people scare me."

By "people", she meant the horde of burly men at almost every entrance point of the sprawling three-storey mansion. So far, we'd estimated that they were guards, but the way they'd looked at us – with menace in their cold eyes – made them seem like serpents in Kevlar.

Mia herself was as scary as they were. Beautiful yet distant, she wore a gorgeous red dress that fell just above her knees. It was skin-tight and showed enough cleavage to feed a pervert's imagination for years to come. I hadn't exactly bothered to dress up. It wasn't standard procedure whenever Megan and I delivered cakes. I usually favoured jeans and a T-shirt. This time, however, I did dress up – moderately. Megan had arched a brow when she'd seen the summer dress I'd pulled on that morning. It wasn't overly sexy or anything, just a bit...womanly. I needed to feel like a woman.

Mia Donafrio's kitchen was bigger than my kitchen and living room combined. The walls were painted a vivid red that set off the black granite countertops and terracotta-hued cupboards running along the walls. A stainless steel state-of-the-art oven stood proudly at one end. Mia motioned for us to place the cakes on the large island in the centre of the kitchen.

"The men are bringing in the rest," she said, bending to get a whiff of one cake. I'd taken my time with this batch. They just had to be perfect, for reasons unknown to me. "Smells good," Mia praised, straightening up.

Megan made murmured excuses and crept away. Honestly, she was behaving as if Mia was the Wicked Witch of the West and she was Dorothy.

"I take it you're the Clarke in Clarke's Cakes?"

I nodded. "Danielle."

She eyed me curiously. "Will you be staying?"

"No, I can't. I –"

"But I insist." Mia licked her lips. Her lipstick did not smudge. "I wouldn't mind a fresh face in the sea of my usual guests."

"I don't think I –"

"I insist." The way she said it made it clear that her word was final. Even if only through marriage, she was an obtuse Donafrio.

I sighed, making sure she knew my answer was reluctant. "All right. Happy birthday, by the way."

She beamed at me. "Grazie. How about you go to the entertainment lounge? I'm sure there are already people there. You should mingle."

I did, after telling Megan that she could leave. She'd given me a startled look.

"Blink three times if you're being held against your will," she'd hissed.

"Really, Meg. You watch too many movies."

Mia had been right – there was a crowd of people clustering around the bar that was set up in her "entertainment lounge". I felt acutely un-derdressed. The women weren't wearing gowns, obviously, seeing as how shockingly hot it was outside, but they did look extremely fashionable. A cotton summer dress certainly stood out like a sore thumb. I suddenly wondered if I should've just emphatically told Mia that I had a prior engagement. In fact, I simply wanted to slink away unnoticed.

But of course, Carlo had to step into the room just then.

I instinctively tried to hide, immersing myself in the sea of chattering people. He would just jump to the wrong conclusion if he spotted me. Besides that, I simply didn't want to see him. He unsettled me.

From my vantage point in a corner, I could see how all the guests flashed him megawatt smiles; shook his hand when he approached them. They didn't seem to experience the stab of fear that was part and parcel of being in Carlo Donafrio's presence. But perhaps they knew how many people he'd murdered and were completely okay with it. For all I knew, all the men in the room were dodgy mobsters and their women cheap hussies.

I must be crazy, I mused, shaking my head.

"Danielle?"

Just my luck.

I forced a smile onto my face. "Carlo, hi."

"What are you doing here?" He formally extended his hand. I looked at it. "You're supposed to take it," he clarified slowly, a smile tugging at one corner of his lips.

Those lips.

His hand swallowed mine and I thought I'd die on the spot. It was hard and warm. I became soft and warm.

"Mia invited me to stay," I garbled, wondering if he could tell how aroused I'd just become because of a handshake. "Trust me when I say that this is the last thing I could've ever wanted."

He released me. "She must like you."

A worry line creased my forehead. "Did you tell her about...you-know -what?"

He shook his head emphatically. "And I don't want you opening your mouth, either." He fixed me with a warning glare.

"I sure as hell won't."

"Good."

"I need a drink," I breathed.

"Allow me," said Carlo, and he turned on his heel to push his way through the people attached to the bar. Actually, he didn't need to do much pushing. They seemed to part like the Red Sea for him.

I watched him go, licking my dry lips. Why was I still standing there? Why wasn't I making a run for it?

"He has a Glock in his pants," I said aloud. "Why are you still standing here waiting for him?"

I shut up as soon as I saw him return. He handed me a flute of champagne.

"Blue is certainly your colour," he said, appraising me.

It felt like I'd somehow been transported back to secondary school by the way I felt heat flush my face.

"Thank you." I gulped down the drink in one swig.

"But you should keep your hair loose," he continued huskily, simultaneously reaching down to remove my hair from its messy ponytail. "It makes a man see what it would look like fanned across a pillow after a session of passionate lovemaking."

"What?" I choked out, gripping the stem of my glass so tightly it was a wonder the thing didn't shatter in my fingers.

"Think about that one."

I was. I was beginning to think about a whole lot of things that had to do with being naked and doing the most sinful things with this man. The memory of his dirty dealings brought me back to earth with an unceremonious thump.

"I'm sorry, but I have to go," I said quickly, pushing past him.

His hand shot out to grip my wrist. "I don't think so."

I glared up at him. "What do you think you're playing at?"

"Forgive me if you're entertaining company, Danielle."

"What do you want from me?"

"Nothing that you don't already want to give me, cara." He slowly let go and I all but ran out the room – and collided into Mia.

"Is everything all right?" she asked, breaking her icy exterior. "You look a little flushed."

"Your...your brother-in-law," I surprised myself by saying, handing my empty glass to a passing server.

"Carlo?" She waved a flippant hand. "He's a hopeless flirt but he means no harm." She took my hand and whispered conspiratorially, "The truth is that he's lonely."

Lonely.

Right.

A lonely murderer-slash-drug dealer-slash-crook.

It was almost ten and Jules had left me several messages suggesting that Mickey might be colicky. It wasn't fair for me to use her as a free babysitter, much as she enjoyed being his godmother. Jules was Jules and staying at home with a screeching baby was far from her list of top things to do over the weekend.

The party was still in full swing and Mia, who'd turned thirty-five, was putting teenagers to shame with her moves like Jagger. Instead of looking trashy, she'd just looked like she was having the time of her life with not a care in the world. I envied her.

"Taxi?" one of the guards grunted once I'd stepped out the front door of the mansion.

"I'll call one, thanks," I told him, rooting into my bag for my mobile.

He didn't say anything else and that was perfectly all right with me.

"I knew you looked sorta familiar," a voice came from behind me.

I whirled around and came face to face with Angelo Donafrio. "Stay away from me, you lying...dog," I finished lamely.

He chuckled, flicking the butt of his cigarette into the bushes by the door. "Did Carlo invite you? Weird, isn't it? Especially with Mia."

"Shut up."

"So what are you guys? A couple? Fúck buddies? Confused?"

It was obvious that he'd been drinking. A prickle of annoyance crept to the fore of my mind.

"I made the dessert, okay? That's what I do. It's not my fault Mia asked me to stay." Why did I feel that I had to explain myself to this scum? Because that's exactly what Angelo was – scum.

"Yeah, and I'm sure you give dessert. If you're waiting for my cousin, don't hold your breath," he said sarcastically. "He was particularly en-twined with some redhead last time I saw him. I, on the other hand..." He took a few steps toward me. "I'm a free agent."

I wrinkled my nose in disgust. "I'd rather touch myself to Dolly Parton."

He laughed hysterically. "I didn't know you had a funny bone in you. May I see your other bones?" He reached for me. I stepped back.

"You're drunk. Go away."

"The human body has two-hundred-and-six bones in it," Angelo slurred, ignoring me completely. "Once I'm inside you, there'll be two-hundred-and-seven."

"Is that really the best you can do, Angie?" Carlo stood on the doorstep, shooting daggers at his cousin.

"I was just messing with her."

Carlo broke into a stream of heavy Italian, all of it going over my head. I'd taken Spanish for my GCSEs and it was far from being close to Italian like my teacher had promised, at least to me.

Angelo seemed to have been heavily berated. He pushed past Carlo on his way back inside, deliberately shoving him with his shoulder.

"Adorable," I said dryly.

"He's family."

"How could I have forgotten?"

"Let me give you a ride home." Carlo nodded towards a car parked on its own under a tree. His BMW.

"I don't think so. Like I said –"

"Your stubbornness is far from endearing, Clarke." He grabbed my arm, tugging me along.

"I don't know what kind of females you associate yourself with," I spat, trying to wrench myself away, "and quite frankly, I don't want to know – but dragging me around like a sack of potatoes is hardly chivalry."

I felt the vibrations of his laugh. "I thought I was a monster and a thug. What do I know about chivalry?" He withdrew his hand and pulled open the passenger door. "Get in."

I stared at him.

"Get in, please," he amended.

So I did. And instantly regretted it when the scent of his cologne permeated my nostrils and skyrocketed my already high blood pressure. Once he was inside too, I found that I could hardly breathe. Well, I could breathe, but every breath I took made everything worse. He seemed to fill the entire car with his presence. If I didn't keel over from cologne-inhalation, I was sure to die of arousal.

This isn't going to be pretty, I thought when the radio came on.

Usually, Pete Tong could relieve all my stress when he was on the radio. But tonight, I barely heard him introduce an exclusive Ed Sheeran track. I barely heard the sound of the car's engine as Carlo shifted into gear and rolled out of the high, steel gates.

"Could we...could we pick Mickey up from my friend's place?" I asked tentatively. "It's near my house. Promise."

"Of course," he replied, keeping his eyes on the road.

"Thanks."

One hand moved from the steering wheel and palmed one of my knocking knees. I hadn't even noticed they were shaking. "Stop it," Carlo said quietly. "You don't have to be afraid of me."

Then remove your hand, I felt like screeching. It burned. It burned in the worst possible way, sending sizzles of pain directly to the warmth between my legs.

As if he'd heard me, he withdrew his hand, shifting gears again.

"But maybe we do need to talk," I blurted out, and he gave me a sideways glance. "You know, about everything. This...this situation."

"Well, we do."

"I'll call Jules and ask her if Mickey could spend the night," I said, feeling like the worst mother on Earth. What if he was colicky?

"So we can talk?" Carlo's eyes were now burning into me.

"Yes," I replied, mind made up. "So we can talk."

Chapter 3

I flicked the light switch on in the living room and gestured for Carlo to take a seat. He pointedly didn't mind me. I froze when his hand came to the small of my back, instantly scorching my skin through the fabric of my dress.

"What are you doing?" I croaked out.

It wasn't as if I was a stranger to a man's touch, but being a single mother was rarely appealing to the run-of-the-mill male, so I could definitely be forgiven for flinching in surprised arousal the way I did. By Carlo's tone, he thought I found his touch unbearably disgusting.

"Talking," was his abrupt response.

My mobile bleated from the depths of my handbag and snapped me out of my trance. I stepped away from Carlo and pulled it out, grateful for the diversion. Jules had finally replied to my text.

It's OK. Turns out he just wanted that stupid bear Charlie bought him. See u tomorrow. x

So she was fine with Mickey spending the night. I shouldn't have been so pleased about that but I was. Mickey certainly shouldn't have been privy to the discussion that was about to take place. Plus, the less he saw of Carlo Donafrio, the better.

I cleared my throat and turned to fix my eyes on the man that was currently invading my space. "Sit," I commanded, knowing that he wouldn't obey me. Obedience clearly wasn't in his vocabulary, unless it was directed to him.

"Is this some sort of strange, coy English girl foreplay?" Carlo questioned, closing the space between us in one step. "I must say, it's...refreshing."

"Foreplay?" I sputtered, noticing how his eyes had turned a shade darker, murkier. "You think I'm... You think I want to... to seduce you?"

"I don't think it, cara. I know it." He firmly cinched his big hands around my waist, drawing me to him in one swift tug.

Of course he would've thought that. In the murky puddle that was my mind, I knew that that's what it had sounded like when I'd invited him in 'to talk'. Obviously he used his mouth for other things after ten p.m.

"But...but..." I stammered, then changed tack. "I'm not your type."

He cocked his head. "No doubt."

I felt myself go cold. "Now that we've clarified that particular bit of information, why don't you let me go?" I said through clenched teeth.

Why are you offended? my conscience wanted to know. It's the truth! You're complete opposites!

"But we are having such a fruitful discussion, Danielle." He dragged my name out; tasting it, making it his.

I pushed at his chest, fighting against the way I was creaming my thong. "You're the one that wanted to talk about my son and I think you're right. I need to set some ground rules here."

He slowly released me and claimed the armchair behind me as his. "Go ahead."

"Good," I said, shocked to learn that I was actually disappointed that I could feel his big hands all over me no longer. It was this cursed dress. It was probably far too short for me and probably had some kind of aphrodisiac built into the hemline. "I'm going upstairs to change," I told Carlo, "and don't follow me."

Before he could say anything, I turned on my heel and bounded up the stairs. Once inside my bedroom, the dress came off and a faded pair of jeans and tatty T-shirt came on. As an afterthought, I stuffed my gun into my back pocket before heading back downstairs.

To my disbelief, Carlo was right where I'd left him. I paused in the doorway, watching him when I was sure he couldn't see me. He really was as good-looking as his picture all those years ago, if I remembered correctly. Thick, wavy hair slightly tousled… The top few buttons of his white dress shirt undone… He looked good enough to eat.

"I don't know about you English, but in my culture, it's rude to stare," he uttered, not even bothering to look at me.

I reddened, shuffling through the doorway. "I don't think it's a good idea for you to be in contact with my son," I told him, getting straight to the point, "and don't try to act like you want to be Father of the Year, either. We both know it's not you."

Carlo stretched his long legs in front of him, majestically reclining in the chair. "Go on."

I didn't want to think about what those legs would look like, bare and exposed against the white of my bed sheets. I didn't want to, but I found that I was thinking about it.

I cleared my throat, briefly tearing my eyes away from him. "I don't want anything to do with you and the clinic; with your legal proceedings. I just want to be left alone." I paused, thinking about it. "Granted, I should be enraged that Mickey has some of your blood in his veins because the clinic didn't want to get rid of what they figured was A-grade sperm – but I just want to get on with my life, okay?"

"I see."

"I also really don't want anything to do with your family," I continued. "Mia's fine, if you look past how scary she comes across at first, but Angelo and God-knows-who-else are as dirty as you are. I don't want to be guilty by association."

"Guilty of what exactly?" His brow was creased in confusion.

"Don't play dumb with me," was my response. "I listen to the news. On that note, if you ever pick my locks again, I will report you to the Parkton Police Station."

"Is that a threat?" he asked menacingly, looking up at me with a slow smile spreading across his face. Despite the fact that I was the one standing, Carlo was the intimidating party.

"I'm glad you find me so amusing but I'm being serious," I spat, folding my arms across my chest. "You can't just waltz into someone's house anytime you please. There are laws against that."

"It's not your house yet," Carlo said quietly. "You're still paying off the mortgage, aren't you?"

"Are you checking me out?" I hissed in disbelief.

"I am, and from down here, I like the view." The smile left his face. "I know you don't think I could possibly care, but let me remind you, Danielle Clarke, that I never asked for this, either. But the fact remains that Michael is half mine and I must ensure that the woman he calls his mother is as she seems."

"Half yours?" I snorted. As if my son was a piece of property to divide... "Don't make me laugh!"

"This is far from a laughing matter," he growled, getting to his feet. I instinctively took two steps back. "What is it?" he barked, eyes blazing. "Do you think I'm going to attack you? Rape you?"

"Don't be ridiculous," I breathed out, sweat trickling down my back. "But I can see that I have royally pissed you off, so if it's all right with you, I'd like you to calm down first before we discuss this like rational adults."

"Is that so?" he said sarcastically. "According to you, I'm nothing but a dangerous criminal. There is absolutely no way a gangster like me can be a rational adult."

I gulped. "I think... I think I've said everything I wanted to say."

"But I haven't," he said in a low voice.

I was the stupid little pig who'd built her house out of straw and made the big, bad wolf's job easier by inviting him inside to gobble me up. The big, bad wolf just happened to be Carlo Donafrio, who'd made me think for just a millisecond that he was a decent human being.

What a laugh.

"What is it, then?" I forced myself to say, the back of my legs bumping the coffee table.

"What are you going to tell him when he's old enough to ask about his father?" Carlo intoned, voice as cold as the look on his face.

"That's funny. Angelo asked me the same thing – right after he lied through his teeth to get into my house and scare me half to death."

"Forget about my cousin for just one second," he snapped. "What will you tell your son?"

Anger seized me. "I'll tell him to look at the Wanted Fugitives section in the local paper, because that's exactly where you'll be!"

His mouth became a thin line. "Dangerous words. Why have you invited me into your home if I'm such a threat?"

"You're not a threat," I lied. "In fact, I pity you. You must have been extremely low on cash to wank into a cup for it, Carlo Donafrio."

"You know I didn't do it for the money," he growled.

"How philanthropic of you!" I sneered, feeling like a vindictive bully in the playground – but Carlo deserved it. How dare he think I wanted to take him to my bed?

I felt the first sharp stab of fear through my heart when Carlo looked at me with thunder in his eyes. That look was a mixture of anger and something else I couldn't quite put my finger on.

"What are you going to do now? Kill me?" I continued, unable to stop goading him. Fingering the 9mm in my back pocket, I remembered that I'd never even shot the damn thing, despite my brothers' constant pleas to teach me. If push came to shove, I'd probably just end up shooting myself like that New Orleans rapper.

Carlo's shadow blanketed me. "Kill you?" His brow furrowed. "Do you really think that lowly of me, cara? I'm wounded."

"Then what the hell do you want?"

His face flashed with a look I barely recognised – pure arousal. Even when he reached out and pulled me to him, I could feel it but couldn't really understand it.

"I realised that the mother of my child is more of a spitfire than I thought." His lips brushed my earlobe. "Call me a pyromaniac."

I tilted my head upwards and eagerly anticipated the touch of his lips, so full and inviting. When it finally came, I threw my arms around his neck and gave him permission to do whatever he wanted with me. It was then that I realised that even from the beginning, this was how I'd wanted the evening to end, with Carlo Donafrio ravaging me completely.

It was a bad idea for me to let this happen, I knew, but why did bad things feel so wonderful? So right? So good?

Carlo's hands gripped the back of my head, his fingers tangling with my unruly hair. A moan escaped my lips when he gently sucked on my bottom lip. His touch sent the most exciting electric shocks through my entire body, making the tiny hairs on my skin stand up. It felt like he was already inside me by the way I became wet.

Has it really been that long? I thought to myself, pressing myself against him. The swell of his erection was now pushed against my abdomen.

"Tell me, Danielle," said Carlo, momentarily removing his mouth from mine. His hands were unbuttoning my jeans. "Are you a screamer?"

"Only if someone makes me," I breathed, nearly pleading with him to hurry it up.

"Challenge accepted."

And he picked me up, hoisting me over his shoulder. Upside down, the blood quickly rushed to my head. I screamed, gripping at the material of his shirt.

"Are you crazy?" I squealed as he carried me upstairs. The steps had never seemed so many until just then.

"Nice room," he remarked, kicking my bedroom door closed behind him.

Finally, he set me down on the bed.

"Don't ever do that to me again!" I fumed, heart thumping against my chest. Something felt wrong. I pressed my rear into the mattress again, then dug into my back pockets. "Where's my –"

"This?" Carlo held my gun up.

I scowled.

He handed it back to me. "I'm confused. Were you going to shoot me if I made one wrong move?"

I sighed, getting up and shoving the bloody thing into the drawer of my nightstand. "I don't know what I was going to do."

"Do you think I'd hurt you?" he asked, coming up behind me.

"Maybe." I let out a hiss of pleasure when he brought his mouth to the side of my neck. "God, everything you do is…" My voice trailed off as I stared at the curtains above the nightstand. What the hell was I saying?

"What?" His arms snaked around me and his hand slid up my T-shirt. "Everything I do is what, cara? Say it."

I thought I'd be even moderately self-conscious about the miniscule zigzags of stretch marks still taking their time to disappear, and the faint scar of my C-section, but I wasn't. In fact, I revelled in Carlo's caress. The pad of his index finger circled my navel, tickling me yet only intensifying the tug of arousal in my abdomen.

I turned around. I had to ask.

"Why do you want me? Why are you here, in my bedroom?"

He swept a hank of hair away from my face. "Because we both don't want to be alone tonight."

There was something in his beautiful emerald eyes that made me want to believe him, that made me want to believe that there was more to the man behind the sordid headlines.

"Baciami," Carlo said softly. "Make the next move."

I wanted to.

I kissed him with a passion I didn't know I possessed. It was a hungry kiss, a desperate one. It was as if his mouth contained the oxygen I needed to breathe and melding our mouths together was the only way for me to get it. Somehow, without my knowing, our clothes came off. I pulled away, wondering if Carlo was just as gorgeous naked as I'd imagined over the past few weeks.

I was shocked to see the scars, the tattoos; the visible evidence of who he really was.

His body was chiselled in all the right places, a fine line of dark hairs leading down to the short, dark curls surrounding his startlingly huge, erect manhood. I dragged my eyes away from it and zoned in on a particularly ugly scar that ran across his side. He had tiny pockmarks on his chest that showed signs of less violent fights, fights in which he'd probably been the victor. Like a graffiti-laden wall, tattoos covered any other bare skin on his upper torso.

"You're afraid," he calmly observed.

"I'm not," I whispered, coming to him. "Just...just curious." I pressed my hand against his heartbeat, over one prominent tattoo. "Who's Milo?"

"He was my brother."

I didn't want to pry.

"And yes, if you were wondering, he was murdered."

My head jerked up. "I wasn't wondering."

"Of course, you were."

I didn't bother correcting his assumption. Instead, I traced my fingers over the scar on his side. He flinched.

I instantly retracted my hand. "It can't still be painful, can it?"

"We're standing naked, cara, and you're touching me. It is painful."

A sly smile spread across my face. "I see. Does this hurt?" Emboldened, I palmed his length, astonished by how hard he was.

Carlo's breathing grew ragged. "And you say I'm the monster."

I got on my tiptoes and placed a kiss on his lips. "I want you, Carlo. Take me."

"Gladly," he rasped, and he pushed me back onto the bed, wrenching the covers aside. He parted my thighs, spreading me wide open, giving me no time to hide myself.

His gaze was feral; his hands warm, and when he knelt between my legs, I had no idea why the usual what-does-he-think-about-my-body thoughts weren't swirling in my mind, ruining everything. They were what had always dampened the mood and made me feel so pathetic, like the

Danielle-with-the-lesbian-mum from high school had never really grown up.

My mind instantly went blank when Carlo's tongue immediately ran along the inside of my thigh, tasting me. It was all I could do not to scream for him to stop, when what I really wanted was for him to lick every inch of me if it would feel as good as his mouth on my inner thigh. I could feel myself getting even wetter, if that was even possible at this point. Carlo's breath was hot against the sensitive skin of my thigh and when he went higher, I could barely keep my control. He reached for a pillow and deftly manoeuvred it beneath my pelvis so that it felt as if I were offering myself to him on a silver platter. Squirming in anticipation, I nearly came there and then when his breath returned to the warmth of my cúnt when he positioned his mouth right above my apex. He grabbed my rear and pulled my hips even closer to his face.

"Stop," I whispered, clutching a fistful of bed sheet. "Oh God, don't stop."

He was licking me, slowly, like an ice-cream. His tongue ran along my swollen clít, tormenting the tight bud of nerves, and then it became frantic, almost greedy, until finally, he plunged it inside me. I arched my back, screaming with the intense pleasure of it all.

"Bloody hell, Carlo, stop," I groaned, not recognising this guttural voice as my own. I was vaguely aware of his hands leaving my arse and then I felt him slide two fingers inside me with no resistance. I was too wet for that, so wet that I could hear the squelching of his fingers fúcking into me.

I didn't want him to stop. I wanted him to keep sucking on my clít until I passed out from pleasure. I wanted him to keep exploring the inner walls of my cúnt with his talented tongue and fingers, and I wanted him to bring me to what I knew was going to be an earth-shattering climax.

I pressed my opening into his face, bucking wildly and feeling the eruption build up inside me like a volcano. He was finger-fúcking me while he drew my clít into his mouth – his teeth gently nibbling at the sensitised bud – and I knew I wouldn't be able to hold back any longer.

"I'm...so...close."

Finally, the explosion came, like a sweet release.

Carlo straightened up, licking his lips. "Delizioso."

I sat up, panting for breath. The órgasm Carlo had just gifted me with had settled it: "Fúck me."

"Ask me nicely, bella mia."

I reached out and gripped his erection in my hand. Warm, throbbing and hard, it took everything in my power to stop myself from pushing him onto his back and getting on top of him. Carlo released a low groan.

"Perhaps you can return the favour," he said in a low growl.

"Oh, I intend to," I murmured, watching him settle beside me.

His c0ck was certainly the biggest I'd ever seen. After all, he was the biggest man I'd ever seen. Lying back against the pillows, Carlo regarded me with open curiosity. Perhaps he thought I wasn't used to sucking men off – which would be the correct assumption. It was far too vulgar, too intimate to even consider. Yet here we were, with me practically gagging for it.

Bending, I ran my tongue along his shaft until I reached his heavy balls, giving them a slow lick as well. He shuddered beneath me, and I persevered, licking my way back to the weeping head. The salty taste of his pre-cum made me wonder what it wounded take to make him lose control, to beg me to stop and not mean it. With both hands wrapped around the base, I claimed Carlo's c0ck as mine, taking as much of him into my mouth as I could.

Carlo hissed, grabbing me by the hair. "Merda, merda, merda..." he chanted, his grip on me becoming painful.

I knew enough to know that that he was cursing and that made me smile as I took him even deeper, until I could feel his head brushing against the back of my throat. I felt him tense as I pulled back, releasing him from my mouth with a pop. Tentatively, I began to pump his c0ck slowly, my saliva and his cum making it easier. As I became more used to what I was doing, I picked up the pace, squeezing his balls in one hand and stroking him with the other. Carlo's hips moved to my rhythm, and when I felt him tense up again, I lowered my mouth onto his head and took him inside once more. He pumped into me more fiercely, his head hitting the back of my throat with more force.

I was going to heave, but the fact that I was making him lose control was such a turn-on it was worth it.

"Merda," he repeated hoarsely, and spurted his cum inside my mouth.

The hot liquid flowed down my throat, most of it trickling down my chin and I sat up, licking the taste of him away. Carlo was breathing heavily beside me, his eyes squeezed shut as if he were sleeping. He looked peaceful that way and I instantly remembered what he'd said to me a week ago: I never sleep.

Without thinking, I leaned in and kissed his forehead. His eyes flew open and he manoeuvred himself onto me.

"I need to know if you feel as good as you look," he whispered, parting my thighs.

He drove himself into me in one brutal thrust and I gasped in surprise, clutching at his broad shoulders. He felt too good to be true buried inside me. His mouth was everywhere – in my neck, on the hard nubs I called nipples, and on my mouth, his tongue duelling with mine – as he continued to pummel into me. When he hit my very core – that sweet spot that made me see stars and constellations – I tightened my legs around his waist, begging him to make me come.

He wasn't gentle – far from it – but I decided I preferred it that way. Rough sex was better than anything I'd ever experienced and it was obviously what he knew best. He murmured in hoarse Italian, his hands melded to my hips as he pulled me to him with his every plunge, and I murmured gibberish back. It was too much at once, far too much for me to endure...

We climaxed together, his mouth drowning out my screams of painful ecstasy.

Sated, he slowly pulled out and lifted his weight off me.

And this is the part where you kick him out and hope you never see him again, my conscience advised, but I was too blissful to entertain her sensibilities.

"You're a very good talker, Danielle," Carlo said, breaking the silence and placing his hand on my thigh. "Have you ever considered public speaking?"

I slapped his hand away.

Chapter 4

"So let me get this straight," said Jules, pausing to vigorously demolish her slice of chocolate sponge cake, "you slept with a man you know you shouldn't have, but you – Miss Holier-than-Thou – don't regret it?"

My attention was momentarily on Megan, who was currently struggling to balance two Styrofoam cups of coffee and four plates of cake on one tray as she wended her way through an obstacle course of tables and chairs. Great girl. Zero efficiency.

"Dani!" Jules snapped her fingers in my face.

"Sorry." I reluctantly fixed my eyes on her. "I was just...thinking."

"Are you ever going to tell me who he is?"

I mimed zipping my mouth shut. It wasn't that Jules couldn't keep a secret; it was just that she would judge me and I'd end up feeling God-awful about my weakness for men with accents and staggering height. If I'd told her about discovering who the sperm donor had been, that would've been another story. Jules was still under the impression that the donor had been a nameless face, someone to thank God for once in a while then forget about until someone inevitably brought up the question of who Mickey's father was.

"Why bother telling me, then?" said Jules, obviously prickled. "And next time you want a one-night stand, think about your poor son and his poor sleep-deprived godmother."

Of course. Motherhood had taught me the most important of lessons: Responsibility.

I was once a ditzy, head-in-the-clouds girl, losing everything I got into my hands. Lunchboxes would be misplaced at school, pencils would somehow find themselves out my pencil case, and I regularly purloined a few from my parents to purchase lost school books.

That used to be me.

Until I literally grew up and realised that I wanted a child more than anything in the world. I wanted the baby, but without the male presence that came with making one and raising it. Naturally, I wasn't thinking clearly at the time, after coming out of a messy relationship with a – now that I'd experienced Carlo – wimpy guy named Tim.

"God, if you get any colder, they'll stick a flag on you and call you Aspen," was his parting shot.

Cold? I'd thought, hurt beyond belief. Am I really cold?

I'd seen the Healey Group's television ad, something to do with a woman holding a big, fat baby and another person saying in the background, "You too can have this."

I'd promptly visited the clinic the next day.

Responsibility.

I was going to be responsible for my actions because that's what responsible people did. They didn't shift the blame onto other people because it was convenient that way; didn't decide to call it "a moment of weakness" because it was an easier explanation. They were liable for their actions, owned up and said: "I slept with Carlo Donafrio because, dammit, I wanted to!"

The fact that we hadn't used anything was beyond foolish on our part but fumbling for a condom had been the last thing on my mind. It was just too bad no one had invented a pill that prevented STDs as well.

"I am thinking about Mickey," I said fiercely, and Jules held her hands up in surrender.

The bell at the door tinkered as someone pushed it open. I looked up and saw Libby come in, a vision in some sort of floral cat-suit with an armful of magazines. Jules followed my gaze and wrinkled her nose in visible revulsion when she saw my friend.

"You forgot to mention that you had a lunch date with Britain's answer to Paris Hilton," she mumbled at me, rubbing her temples with her index fingers.

"Hi!" Libby sang brightly, setting what turned out to be bridal magazines on our table. Her eyes flickered to Jules as if she'd only just noticed her sitting opposite me. "Oh. You."

It bothered me that Jules and Libby didn't get along. It had been this way since secondary school and I couldn't, for the life of me, figure out why. So, like the rope in a weird game of tug-of-war, I was inevitably caught in the middle.

"Yes. Me," Jules said curtly. Her sky-blue eyes flashed with a controlled anger. "Are you getting married, or are you playing pretend?" she asked, glancing at the mags.

Libby took the chair at my right, swishing her hair as she sat. "Didn't you know?" She held up her engagement ring finger.

Jules snorted. "Contrary to what your big head might think, the world does not revolve around Libby Wilson. Because there's fúck all going on with you."

"Jules," I said, letting out a sigh. I turned to Libby, trying to diffuse the situation before it got out of hand. "Coffee, Lib? Tea? A latte? Anything?"

"Oh, and what have you got to show for yourself, Jules?" She was completely ignoring me. I hated it when these two went for each other's throats like rabid dogs.

"Oh, I don't know," Jules replied sarcastically, playing with a lock of long, strawberry-blonde hair. "A pretty decent job as editor-in-chief of a more than decent magazine, real tits and – hmmm – an English degree. The only degree you've ever gotten was from your dad, when he gave you the third degree for fúcking your boyfriend in his house on your sixteenth birthday."

There was an uncomfortable silence that followed. The coffee shop wasn't that busy – it was, after all, three o'clock – so there was minimal racket. It still felt like Jules, Libby and I were alone.

"My tits are real," Libby finally spoke through clenched teeth.

"Could you two grow up for just one second?" I muttered, getting annoyed. "You're behaving like pre-schoolers."

"She hasn't changed one bit," was Jules' defence.

"I don't get how you can stand her obnoxious presence," Libby put in.

"Ooh, obnoxious? Spell it."

"Shove your degree up your flat arse!"

Once they started, it was difficult to prise them apart. All I could do was keep my fingers crossed that they wouldn't graduate from a good tongue lashing to something physical. I decided to let them have it out, and rose from the table, heading to the front. Megan was busy with a customer, making a right mess of the change as usual. Sighing, I went round and helped her out.

"I was never good at maths," she said apologetically, running a hand through her mane of hair.

"That's okay."

"No, it's not, Danielle. You're so kind."

I smiled. "Or I might just find you too adorable to fire."

"Oh, and don't think I don't know you're seeing Charlie!" screamed Libby, drawing concerned looks from people at a table a long way from hers.

"What's that got to do with you?" Jules screeched.

"How do you like my sloppy seconds, you dirty slag?"

"You're Charlie's mystery girlfriend?" I called to Jules before I could stop myself.

Jules tore her gaze from Libby, standing up. "Could I please explain?"

The front door was pushed open again and a small cluster of schoolchildren poured in. I signalled Megan to take over and was about to return to my friends when Angelo crept in, fully covered at last in a ridiculously tight-fitting pair of black snakeskin pants and a flamboyant custard-coloured shirt.

"May I speak with you?" he asked politely, cutting in front of the children, who let him pass with no protest.

"I'm busy."

He whirled around. "Kids, how would you like to get outta this dump and cross the road to McDonald's? Here. Spoil yourselves." He rooted in his pockets and pulled out a wad of notes, handing them to the tallest girl in the group.

"Thanks, mister," all six of them sang in unison, turning on their heels and exiting my coffee shop.

I balled my hands into fists. "Who the hell do you think you are?"

He turned to fix his eyes on me. "Now you're free. Come on. Walk with me."

"I will not."

"Is everything okay, Danielle?" came Jules, suddenly appearing beside Angelo.

He gave her an appreciative once-over. "Oh, hello. You a friend of Dani's?"

"Everything's fine, Jules," I snapped.

"If this is about Charlie and me, I was going to –"

"It's fine."

Libby took that opportunity to saunter out the door, leaving her magazines on the table. Clearly she didn't want to come to blows with Jules because Jules would definitely win that fight.

"You're fine, sweetie," Angelo said flirtatiously, his eyes becoming predatory as he blatantly ogled my best friend.

Jules' brow creased. "Sweetie? If you get any slimier, honey, you'll turn into an amphibian. Now, see you later, Dan. Love you."

"Cute friend," Angelo commented, watching her sashay out the door.

"What do you want?"

He sighed. "Maybe we got off on the wrong foot, cupcake."

"I'm just trying to forget ever meeting you."

"See, that's the problem. If you think this is the last you'll see of me, think again." He leaned forward. "Fúcking my cousin kind of makes you a liability."

Heat enflamed my cheeks. "Get out."

"Maybe you think Carlo's gonna dump all the broads he has on his speed dial," Angelo continued, tapping his fingertips on the counter. "Maybe you think he'll want to settle down, become a father – maybe even marry you – but listen here, bakery girl, that won't happen. Blood looks after blood, and I'm looking out for my cousin. Do yourself a favour and stop chasing danger."

I was momentarily stunned. Momentarily.

"I don't want a relationship with him. Quite frankly, I'd be content if you both disappeared into thin air and never came back," I said quietly. "I don't know if he sent you or not, but you can both go fúck yourselves."

His face became granite. "I see you for what you are – a puttana. It was a mistake for me to go looking for you, but I had to make sure you would never go looking for Carlo. You know, once your bastard was all grown up and asking about his daddy."

Bastard, I thought furiously, adrenaline instantly fuelling what I would do next. He called my son a bastard.

The coffee machine was always on. It took exactly two seconds for me to grab and fling a Styrofoam cup of boiling hot coffee at Angelo's face. I had never heard a grown man squeal before but that's exactly what Angelo did. Stumbling backward with his face buried in his hands, he bumped into an empty table and chairs, tripping over them and upsetting the table. The few customers remaining in the café openly stared in disbelief.

"The next time I see you, I'm shooting you in the groin," I called, watching him wobble to his feet.

"Oh, you fúcking slut... You... fúcking... puttana!" he groaned, yelling out the last word at the top of his lungs. "I hope you know how to protect your baby!"

My blood went cold. Angelo staggered out the door, slamming it behind him. I was in my car seconds later to get to the babysitter's.

For as long as I can remember, Adam and Charlie had dreamt of owning a construction company together. They both loved the feel of creating something from scratch with nothing but a vision and their hands and today, Clarke's Construction had its offices three streets away from my café. I was banking on them being there so early on a Saturday morning so as I turned into the driveway and rolled into the parking lot, I looked out for either Adam's silver Merc or Charlie's black Ford truck.

I breathed a sigh of relief when I saw that Adam's car was neatly parallel-parked beside an ancient Toyota sedan. I parked on its other side, getting out and pulling open the backseat door. Mickey was in his car seat, waggling a rattle in one chubby hand.

"That's right, love. We're going to see your uncle Adam," I cooed, tickling him under his chin as I picked him up and balanced him on my hip.

Not for the first time, I admired the office building from the outside. Adam and Charlie had built it themselves. They'd argued about the design and had finally compromised – Adam got his red-brick walls and Charlie had managed to twist his arm into an allowance for glass ceilings. Somehow, the combination worked.

"Morning, Danielle," their receptionist, a gorgeous Irish girl called Lucy, greeted me as soon as I stepped through the entrance. "And hello, Mickey sweetheart."

"Hi. I saw Adam's car outside. Is he in?" Sometimes he'd take a company car to a site, so I couldn't be too sure.

"Yes, but Charlie's on site somewhere."

"That's okay." I walked past her and knocked on Adam's office door.

"Come in." He looked up from the blueprints spread out on his desk and smiled. "What a brilliant surprise, Mick. I was starting to think your mum had put you on the black market."

"Very funny," I said dryly, feeling the familiar warm liquid – Mickey's dribble – seeping into my shoulder as he gurgled. "Is it National No-T-shirt Day?"

Adam flexed, nodding at the mini gym in one corner of the room that consisted of little more than a rubber-coated dumbbell and an ancient elliptical machine.

"Beats going to that stupid Virgin gym down the street," he said, shrugging.

"Right."

"Is everything okay, Dani?" He was giving me his full attention now. "Is it Donafrio? He's hounding you, isn't he?"

I felt like laughing at that one. Hounding me? I hadn't so much as caught a whiff of that man since I'd behaved so wantonly and allowed him into my bed. But that was quite all right with me. I wasn't the type of woman who went out and looked for one-night stands – flings were more my thing – but I didn't exactly regret being with Carlo for one second. Now there was a man who knew the many uses of a mouth.

Of course I didn't say that to my brother. Adam was many things but I got the feeling that he still saw me as a little girl with pigtails and Teletubbies pyjamas. Hearing about my sex life would give him a premature heart attack.

"He's not hounding me," I replied.

"Then what's up? Is Mickey OK?" He gave his nephew a worried look. "You haven't taken him to the doctor, have you?" He let out a sigh. "Dani, I think it's time you –"

"I need you to take me to the shooting range," I cut in, knowing where this was going to go if I didn't stop him. "Please."

Mickey was becoming restless in my arms. Crouching, I set him on the carpet and left him to his own devices. I straightened up just in time to catch the odd look Adam was giving me. "What?"

"The shooting range. I've been asking you to go with me for years and you've been refusing – but as soon as that crook steps on the scene, you realise that it's essential for you to know how to shoot a gun?" His brow creased. "What did he do? Threaten you? Threaten Mickey?"

"Would you stop leaping to conclusions? Can't I just want to protect myself?"

"Well, what the hell am I supposed to think, Danielle?" Adam snapped. "Carlo Donafrio is a dangerous criminal. Quite frankly, I'm astonished how shitty our legal system is, allowing him to walk around as if he's God's gift to psychopaths."

He wasn't a psycho. No, the psycho was his cousin I was itching to shoot.

"What happened to innocent until proven guilty?" I asked. It was a reasonable question but Adam acted as if I'd told him that paedophiles were misunderstood caregivers.

"Carlo? Innocent?" He gave me a suspicious stare. "Dani, is there something you're not telling me?"

If Charlie were here, he'd have been able to guess that I'd slept with Carlo. That was just the way he was, the way he'd always been when it came to me. He could tell if I was lying through my teeth in a heartbeat.

I shook my head, although there were a lot of things that I wasn't telling him, like how it wasn't Carlo I was afraid of, but his nutjob cousin.

Adam sighed. "I know you. You're lying."

"Caro," a voice said below me.

Adam and I both looked down. Mickey was staring up at me with an amused expression on his round face, as if he'd just told the funniest joke and was waiting for us to laugh with him.

"Did he...did he just say –"

"Caro," Mickey repeated, now puzzled that we weren't ecstatic over his little speech.

He knew how to say roughly three words: Mama, chew, and dog.

Now he'd learned a fourth, albeit a bastardised version of it.

Adam shook his head, striding around his table and coming to crouch before his nephew.

"Mickey? That is a bad word," he said in a sing-song voice. "Very bad word."

"Oh, stop it," I said, rolling my eyes.

Adam looked up at me. "Either he's trying to say Carlo, or your son is in Italian 101 and has learned how to say 'dear'. Pick one."

"God, Adam, could you be any more dramatic? Now, will you take me to the range, or shall I go by myself?"

"Fine," he said, getting to his feet. "But if I were you, I'd wash Mickey's mouth out with soap."

I couldn't have been asleep for more than half an hour when I woke up with a start in the blanket of darkness. Instinctively, I felt that something wasn't quite right.

The shadow hovering over Mickey's crib confirmed it.

Everything in me told me to scream but what good would that have done, except to make whoever it was angry enough to kill my son? As quietly as I could, I reached under my pillow and grabbed my pistol, slowly sliding out of bed. Disengaging the safety like Adam had taught me, I fumbled to pull back and load the bullet in the chamber.

The sound was going to scare Mickey; it was going to scare me, but there was nothing else to do.

In the faint moonlight, I could see that whoever it was had just lowered Mickey back into the crib. I didn't want to think about what they had just done to him. Taking aim and saying a silent prayer, I pulled the trigger.

Mickey instantly came to life, his cries starting quietly at first then building momentum.

"Cristo," the person grunted, staggering away from the cot. I took that opportunity to dash to pick up my baby. Mickey's crying instantly stopped short.

"It's okay, it's okay," I said soothingly, rocking him in my arms.

"What the hell is wrong with you, Danielle?"

I recognised that voice. Backing away and flicking on my bedside lamp, the dull glow of the light revealed Carlo. He had one hand on his right bicep, stemming the blood flow.

"What the hell are you doing here?" I screeched, aware that I was in nothing more than Tim's old football T-shirt.

"What are you doing shooting me?" he growled, his face a picture of annoyance.

"I thought you were... I thought you were Angelo."

Carlo sat at the foot of my bed, painfully shrugging out of his sports jacket. "Angelo? What is your obsession with him?"

I returned Mickey to his crib, kissing the top of his head. "Obsession? What on earth are you talking about?"

"Nothing," he bit out. "Get me a towel."

I glared at him. "Get you a towel? Where do you think you are, the Sheraton?"

He glared back. "Actually, the hospital would be a better choice, but understandably, I can't show my face there with a bullet lodged in my goddamn shoulder."

Oh God.

"I...I thought it just grazed you."

"Stop selling yourself short. You have amazing aim," he said wryly, taking his hand away from the wound. The right side of his white T-shirt was stained crimson. "You'll have to remove the bullet."

"How are you not passing out?" I squeaked.

"Danielle. Bullet. Out. Now," he said through gritted teeth.

"OK, OK. What do I need?"

"Do you have any whiskey?"

I nodded.

"Good. That's for me." He smiled. "And I bet you have a whole variety of knives, sì? You badass."

"I...well, kitchen knives, obviously."

"Good. I need one. I have a lighter in my jacket."

"Isn't it better if we leave the bullet inside?" I asked, staring at the rivulet of blood that was now trickling down his arm.

"I know what I'm doing. You just get what I asked for."

Good job, Dani. Now you're going to be playing Dr. Quinn, Medicine Woman at two in the morning, I thought as I bounded down the stairs. Pleased with yourself?

I was far from pleased. It wasn't as if Carlo was in the wrong, either. He'd broken into my house again and I was well within my rights to gun him down like the criminal he was.

After finding an unopened bottle of Jack Daniel's, a small blade, and an old kitchen towel, I left the kitchen and headed back upstairs. Carlo had ripped off his T-shirt – literally ripped it off – and had his hand pressed over the bullet hole, waiting for my return.

"Do you want me to numb the area first?"

He shook his head. "Just get it over with." He reached out for the whiskey, deftly opened it with one hand, and proceeded to down half the bottle.

I knelt beside him, swallowing. Blood didn't make me queasy but digging around in someone's flesh for a bullet probably would.

"Dig it out, Danielle," Carlo was saying.

"Wouldn't a hospital be –"

"Dio mio, you are such a woman," he barked, reaching for the knife himself.

I held it back, my resolve strengthening. "I wouldn't say such things if I were you." Wiping away the blood around the wound as best as I could, I took a deep breath. And began to pry the bullet out. "You'd better hope I don't cut any important veins."

Carlo barely made any noise, save for the occasional Italian profanity under his breath.

Finally, I gingerly picked the bloody bullet out and let out a sigh of relief. Carlo briefly glanced at the gash and doused it with whiskey, wincing.

"Okay, heat up the blade."

"Wait, what?"

"To close the wound. Heat the blade."

"I could just stitch it up."

"Danielle. Blade. Now."

"Fine, fine." I rooted in the pockets of his jacket and found his lighter. Holding it under the knife, I clicked until a bluish flame began to heat the metal. "You owe me for this."

"I owe you?" he snarled. "You're the one who shot me!"

"Don't raise your voice. Mickey's sleeping."

"I'm not – Dammit," he groaned when I pressed the heated blade against his skin. He was silent after that, taking a swig of whiskey. "You enjoyed that, didn't you?" he asked me when it was over.

"Which part? Shooting you, or practically mutilating you? So much to choose from."

He examined my handiwork. "Do you have any gauze?"

I got to my feet and pulled the first aid kit from under my bed, digging inside until I found a roll of thick gauze. Carlo allowed me to wrap it around his arm, running his hand over it when I was done.

"You're good," he remarked.

"Oh, you know, knife wounds are my specialty, but bullet wounds are almost the same," I said sarcastically, collecting the tatters of his T-shirt and the bloody towel. I paused. "Carlo, what exactly were you doing? It's almost two a.m."

He flexed his arm. "I was in the neighbourhood."

"Bullshit."

A smile tugged at his lips. "Fine. I couldn't sleep."

"So you broke into my house?"

"Like I said, cara, you need new locks."

"What were you doing with my son?"

"He was awake when I came in. Why have you moved him out of the nursery?"

Because I'm scared your crazy cousin's going to come after him.

Something hit me. "Do you come here often? When I'm asleep?"

It suddenly made sense, even before he answered my question. Mickey wasn't waking me up at night any longer, which was unusual, when he was such a terrible sleeper. I'd just put it down as fatigue, but maybe... Then there was his sudden grasp of Carlo's name...

"You won't let me see him during the day," Carlo said quietly. "This is my compromise."

"Your compromise?" I sputtered. "You're not entitled to anything! You don't get to make compromises. You're not his father."

He rose. "This might come as a shock to you, Danielle, but I do care about him. Let me remind you that I would never have wanted this either, but he is a Donafrio. That won't change."

He wants an heir.

Charlie's words reverberated in my skull once more. I became panicked, my heart doing a frantic dance in my ribcage. It suddenly dawned on me that he wouldn't be a nameless face again. Ever.

"I want you to get out," I told him. "I'll get a restraining order, whatever it takes. Just leave us the hell alone."

"You don't want to go the legal route with me, Danielle," he said menacingly.

"No, I don't," I told him, the wheels in my head turning frantically. There was only one way to stop his train of thought... I wasn't above doing it. "I think you know which route I do want to go with you," I said softly. "The one that leads to my shower."

"Non capisco," he said to himself, arching a brow. "I don't understand."

I ran my hands over his chest and kissed him. "You have to wash this blood off. Let me help."

He kissed me back, even more viciously, his lips bruising mine. I pressed myself against him, reaching into his pants to feel the length of his c0ck.

Sometimes, I thought as I led him to my bathroom, a woman has to bargain with her body.

It didn't hurt that I still wanted him to fúck me.

Chapter 5

He was a man.

No matter how arrogant or timid, dangerous or docile they were, men thought about sex more than they thought about more pressing issues – like veiled threats about taking someone's child away.

Carlo certainly wasn't any different.

"Slow down," I breathed, after having the wind knocked out of me when he pushed me up against one ceramic wall. "Weren't you just shot an hour ago?"

Carlo cast a dismissive look at his bandaged arm. "I'll live." His eyes roamed over me. "But you should know that I'm not lenient with my attempted murderers and there have been many."

I couldn't be sure if he was teasing or not. "Are you threatening me? Because I'll –"

"You'll what?" He leaned in and blew his hot breath against the sensitive skin of my neck. "Tell your brothers?" His tongue flickered out and traced one of the cords of my neck. "The cops?" I felt his teeth, gentle yet painful because of the sweet sensation they caused. "Your little girlfriends?" He bit down. I let out a helpless whimper.

"You can't just waltz into my house whenever you feel like it," I said softly, shuddering when his hand slid up my T-shirt and forgetting the rest of what was going to be a passionate tirade.

"I think, cara," he murmured into my neck, "that you'll find that I can do whatever the hell I please." He reared back, tugging my top off with one hand.

I wasn't wearing any underwear. After my shower before bed, I'd just thrown on a shirt because of the slight rise in temperature. Now it just looked like an invitation, something I was banking on.

"There is something I have to ask – something I should have asked the moment we had sex the first time," Carlo was saying, his eyes decidedly settling on my breasts. "Are you taking any contraceptives?"

"Of course I am," I snapped indignantly, the trance broken. "What sort of idiot do you take me for? Do you honestly think I'd –"

He covered my mouth with his hand, wincing slightly from the pain he most likely experienced to lift his bandaged arm. His free hand cupped my breast, the pad of his thumb over my nipple, and both my breasts suddenly felt like the heaviest of boulders.

"I don't think you're an idiot," he whispered, "because I am. Christo, Danielle! I have never been so careless when it came to protection. Never."

You and me both, I thought to myself.

"Are we just going to talk?" I said aloud, letting my fingers trace the contours of his ruined chest.

He trembled from my touch, his top lip curling. "Di niente. We're not going to talk."

I looped my arms around his neck and he leaned in to kiss me. Carlo Donafrio might have been a shady miscreant but he certainly knew how to make a woman overly excited with that tongue of his. Grabbing the back of my head with one hand, he pressed himself against me and I winched myself up his powerful frame and wrapped my legs around his waist.

He whirled me around, not breaking our kiss, and pointed me in the direction of the bathtub. I was vaguely aware of his stepping into the empty tub and then I hopped off, giving him a searching look.

"The bathtub, Carlo? Really?" I reached for him and unzipped the fly of his pants, which he wordlessly shucked and flung onto the linoleum floor. He was wearing silk boxers and they masked an impressive erection. It was still extremely fascinating to know that I was responsible for his arousal. Me, with my stretch marks and close-to-dangling tits.

"The shower's overrated," he explained, lowering himself down and leaning back, daring me to join him. My pússy was now eye-level to him and it throbbed in anticipation. I obliged.

Carlo inhaled sharply when I tentatively eased his c0ck out. "Merda," he hissed, squeezing his eyes shut. "Fúck me, Dani Clarke. Fúck me."

If anyone had told me that Carlo Donafrio would be in my empty bathtub at two in the morning groaning for me to "fúck him", I would've checked that person into the nearest mental facility. As it was, I was turned on beyond possible belief and everything in my head that said this was so, so wrong simply withered away and became nothing.

I wanted him and I didn't care how.

There was no need for foreplay. I'd been more than ready for him since he'd ripped off his shirt to let me clean his wound. Without breaking eye contact, I reached behind me and turned on the hot and cold water taps. Carlo's eyes never left mine – until I spread my legs, hanging one over one side of the tub. The sight of his eyes on my pússy was making me wetter by the second. I wanted to be dirty – forget the consequences, forget the situation – but I also wanted to make him forget.

Forget about ever trying to take my son away from me.

I flipped the taps off. "Touch me." My voice was breathless, hungry.

Carlo's eyes had darkened with desire to something close to coal-black. He reached out for me. "Come here, mia strega."

"What does that mean?"

His eyes were glazed as he murmured, "Witch. You have bewitched me, Dani mia."

Dazed with need, I moved to sit astride him without lowering myself onto his c0ck. Angling my head, I leaned in and placed a light kiss on the side of his neck. My tongue flickered out and I slid it down his neck and onto his collarbone.

"Stop," he grunted.

"Imagine that this is your c0ck," I hissed, and sucked on a bit of flesh, nibbling on his spicy skin.

Carlo's hands came around me as I moved to lick one of his caramel-coloured nipples. They were hard and for some reason, that just did it for me. And him.

He thrust upwards and our bodies were perfectly joined. I sat still for a few minutes, just enjoying the feel of him inside me, and then it became agonising.

Slowly, I began to move my hips while Carlo threw his head back and released the softest of groans. He was exercising self-control while I took control and to me, that was both generous and astonishing. Leaning forward and raising my arse up and down, I felt his manhood slide even deeper inside me, hitting my inner walls. Carlo filled me up entirely and I could already tell that my orgasm was going to be sensational, was going to destroy me.

"Dio mio," he groaned, his fingers leaving dents in my backside. "You will be the death of me, cara mia."

I placed my head on his chest, the thump of his racing heartbeat vibrating against my forehead. Mouth pressed to his chest now, I moaned freely, not wanting to make any noise that might awaken Mickey.

Carlo's hands were now firmly cinched on my thighs, gripping them tightly as I rode him with abandon. I was becoming frantic, trying to reach the end result of this game – the big O.

He raised his hips, easing into my rhythm as he thrust into me. I squeezed my legs together, contracting my inner walls and tightening myself around him. Carlo's sounds of pleasure weren't as easy to muffle as mine. I was going to explode anytime soon.

"I'm going to…" I gasped, trailing off.

"I know." He picked up the pace, even as I threw my head back and came, my juices flowing from the floodgates themselves.

When he eventually climaxed, I finally understood the meaning of the phrase "having the life squeezed out of you". If he really wanted, Carlo could snap my neck between his thumb and index finger, so it wasn't a surprise that when he came, the sheer force of his ejaculation was enough to tear a scream from me.

"Did I hurt you?" he breathed when it was over and all I could manage was a soft sigh of contentment as I collapsed onto him.

"No," I lied.

He kissed my forehead. "You are a bad liar and I am sorry."

I was alone in my bedroom when I woke up.

No Mickey.

No Carlo.

He stayed the night? I thought hysterically, mentally slapping myself as I kicked the tangle of sheets off and grabbed my nightgown. His scent filled the room, as did the smell of heated sex. *Carlo Donafrio spent the night in my bed?*

Fear spidered up my spine. Yes, Mickey's crib was empty and yes, the faint impression on the right side of my bed told me that Carlo had definitely spent the night.

And now they were both gone.

"Don't panic, Dani," I told myself, panicking. How stupid could I have been to trust him? For what, really mind-blowing sex? Was that all it took to buy my only child?

I practically flew down the stairs, biting my bottom lip as I frantically dashed outside to see if I could find any clues – like Mickey's favourite toy, a gift from Charlie, which could've dropped as Carlo had rushed him to his car and sped off to a place where he was immensely powerful and I was a nobody with no rights.

Jumping to conclusions, aren't we, Dani?

True. They could've walked.

But Carlo's BMW was still parked in my driveway.

Turning on my heel, I went back inside – and heard familiar gurgling coming from the kitchen.

"Mickey?" I whispered as I approached the doorway of the kitchen.

With a sigh of relief, I saw that he was sitting on the floor at Carlo's feet in a fresh playsuit, playing with his teddy bear. I couldn't say I was relieved to find a topless Carlo at my stove, his back to me.

"I hope your mother likes her eggs scrambled, figlio mio," he was saying, and the smell of eggs finally wafted into my nostrils, eliciting a rumble from my stomach.

Mickey babbled some sort of response as if they were having an actual conversation and he was giving his very valued opinion.

Carlo looked down at him. "What was that, caro? You think she'll find some reason to throw it in my face?" he asked. "Smart boy. I bet your mother – who is rudely eavesdropping as we speak – is already planning a way to kick me out."

I felt heat stain my cheeks as I shuffled into the kitchen. "Eavesdropping? This is my house. I can't be accused of eavesdropping in my house."

"Right," he said dismissively, turning back to the pan on the stove. "Sit."

"I had no idea you were so domesticated," I commented dryly, glancing at the plates on the table. "Did they teach Home Economics after Drug Trafficking 101 at your school?"

He spun around, murder in his emerald eyes. In that moment, he looked several shades of dangerous. "Don't talk about things you can't even possibly begin to understand!"

"Don't raise your voice at me in my own bloody house!" I countered.

"I will speak to you however I want to when you disrespect me with your wild, idiotic accusations."

"Don't even pretend to be a saint, Carlo," I snapped. "You and I both know –"

"You know nothing!"

My eyes swivelled down to Mickey, whose eyes were agog with childlike bewilderment. I gave him a small smile and shut up before locking eyes with Carlo.

If looks could kill, I'd have R.I.P. on my forehead.

"You're scaring him," I said softly, and his eyes went to Mickey as well.

"Caro," said Mickey, raising his arms in a bid to be picked up.

"Not again," I muttered, watching as Carlo bent to scoop up my son. "Did you teach him that word?"

"What? Caro?" he asked, settling Mickey somewhere on his hip.

"Yes, that word."

"Not exactly."

"Not exactly?"

Mickey was tugging at a lock of Carlo's curly, jet-black hair and he was paying him no mind. In that moment, I knew that he did love my son – or, at least had a soft spot for him. I had nothing to fear where Mickey was concerned. It was only my life I had to worry about.

Thank God for small mercies.

"Ssh," he hissed, cocking his head to one side. "Did you hear that?"

I listened. "Hear what?"

He thrust Mickey at me. "What did I tell you about getting new locks?"

"What are you talking about?" I held Mickey to me.

Carlo's eyes implored me. "Take him and go upstairs. Lock yourselves in the spare room and don't come out until I tell you to."

"What the hell are you on about?"

"Do you trust me?"

"Not one bit."

He scowled, a tic in his jaw. "Trust me just this once. Get upstairs."

I gave him a puzzled look but turned on my heel and went upstairs, doing exactly as he'd told me. Mickey was becoming restless, though, and I was going out of my mind not knowing what the hell was going on. I let him crawl about while I went to the window and peeked outside.

A black SUV was conspicuously parked outside my gate.

Seconds later, I heard the gunshots.

Chapter 6

"Dani, is this a bullet hole?" Jules burst out, picking up my toaster and whirling around to shove it under my nose.

"What? Of course not. It's a drilling hole. I was starting the...redesigning. It was an accident," I explained quickly, snatching the toaster from her and ushering her back to her seat at my kitchen table. "Tea, right? No milk, one sugar."

Jules' eyes narrowed. "I'm not an idiot, Danielle Clarke."

"I didn't –"

"Do you honestly expect me to believe that you'd been saving up for all of this?" She gestured at my new and improved kitchen. It was something straight out of a magazine. "How stupid do you think I am?"

"Well, you haven't said a word about it for three weeks," I muttered feebly, averting my eyes.

Three weeks.

It was hard to believe that my kitchen and living room had been turned into Swiss cheese exactly three weeks ago; three weeks since I'd seen my first dead body.

Carlo had been standing over the man – whose brains had been so artfully spattered against my television and carpet – and he raised his head to look at me, his gun still in his hand. Splotches of blood were on his chest that were evidence of a close-range shot. He'd obviously had the chance to get up close to whoever the man was and point his gun at his forehead.

"I'm sorry," Carlo had said quietly.

Just like that. "I'm sorry".

"Sorry for what?" I'd felt like screaming. "For sleeping over? For trying to make me breakfast? For attracting random gun-toting men to my house and gunning one down in my fucking lounge?"

But no.

I wished I could say that I'd asked that sort of questions, instead of doing what I did, which was launching myself at Carlo like a rabid Rottweiler and giving him all the venom in my fists. Where was the logic in punching someone for killing someone else in your home? Carlo had barely flinched, just stood there, letting me call him every name in the dictionary while I'd wondered how long it would be until the nosy old hag next door would call the police to report hearing gunshots from my house.

Finally, when I'd lost my energy and acquired some sense of dignity, I crumpled to the floor beside the body and just cried. Crying wasn't something I did often. It was saved for Titanic or The Notebook- moments, or when I got frustrated because I couldn't shut Mickey up.

I'd never had an I've-got-a-corpse-in-my-house-and-I-don't-know-what-to-do cry. Hell, I'd never even seen a corpse before, especially one with half its head missing.

"Dani," Carlo had said soothingly. "Dani, stop crying." He'd knelt before me and pulled me into an embrace. "They were after me, not you."

"And that's supposed to make me feel better?" I'd sobbed, which was a huge mistake because I got blood from his chest onto my lips, instantly tasting copper and coughing.

"Mark my words, I will find out who sent this man," he'd said sharply, "but you can't stay here any longer, cara. For Mickey's sake."

I'd pulled away from him, the tears instantly evaporating. "If this was some sick ploy you concocted with that twat of a cousin of yours to scare me, you can both go fúck yourselves."

Carlo cursed in Italian. "What are you talking about?"

"Ask Angelo!"

Carlo's face had hardened. "How many times have you seen him behind my back?"

"Behind your back?" I'd repeated incredulously.

"What? Do you expect to play the both of us with your –"

My hand had been itching to make its acquaintance with his cheek and it felt invigorating to finally oblige it.

"Fúck you," I'd snarled, getting to my feet before he could. "I don't want either of you! You can clean up this mess because...because I don't want any part of this."

If I'd thought my living room had been a disaster zone, my kitchen had been far worse. Every surface had holes in it and glass shards had covered the linoleum floor. My windows had been completely shattered. The house I was working up to owning was as broken as I felt inside. I wanted to cry.

After I'd gone back upstairs to check on Mickey, who was fast asleep in his cot, I'd slipped into the shower and tried to wash as much of Carlo – as well as the dead man's blood – off me.

What was I thinking? I'd thought, scrubbing down until my skin was painfully raw.

If I needed any more reason not to associate myself with the Donafrio family, the dead body in my living room was more than enough to convince me that breaking all ties with them was in my and Mickey's best interests. Besides that, who the hell did Carlo think he was to assume that I could possibly be interested in his degenerate cousin, especially after his blatant threats?

He doesn't give a rat's arse about Mickey.

When I'd returned downstairs, the body had disappeared and a tall, bald-headed man had been standing at the door.

"Mr. Donafrio said to tell you that there'll be an interior designer coming in tomorrow," he'd told me monotonously. "I'm Gav. I'll be the guy ensuring that what happened today doesn't happen again."

"You mean, like a bodyguard?"

"I'll be the Kevin Costner to your Whitney." His face had been chillingly deadpan.

Three weeks later and Gav was still unobtrusively watching my house. If Jules or either of my brothers ever caught wind that Carlo had hired a bodyguard for me, there would be hell to pay. There'd be far too many questions and few believable answers. Charlie would form a one-man attack on the Donafrio family and would probably die in the process, a martyr because of my own stupidity.

Dragging myself to the present, I gave my best friend a sober look. "Jules, I had been saving for this," I said as emphatically as I could, although the look on her face told me that she thought I was spewing bullshit. "Adam said it's impressive." Well, his actual words had been: "Oh, sis. Tell me you didn't make an impressive deal with the devil." Apparently, he believed that I could sell my soul for a stainless steel, double-door Samsung refrigerator and numerous Russell Hobbs kitchen appliances.

What would he say about my mortgage being paid off?

Carlo was a billionaire so a simple renovation and a few thousand pounds in credit was small change to him. There was no reason for me to feel guilty. Besides, it was his fault I'd needed to redecorate.

Jules shook her head. "You might've been able to fool your brothers but you can't fool me."

I sighed. "I'm not fooling anyone."

"Right," she said sarcastically, "and I suppose you're going to tell me that the skinhead lurking about is a figment of my wild imagination?"

Jules Nelson just wasn't going to give up.

"I hate this colour," I muttered, pushing aside the curtain of the changing room and twirling so Libby could see how ridiculous I looked. I was positive that the young sales assistant was laughing behind her perfectly composed mask of patience.

Libby clapped her hands together, glancing at the sales assistant, whose nametag proclaimed that she was Zoe. "Don't be silly. Doesn't she look adorable?"

Zoe nodded her assent, knowing better than to actually speak. Libby was a chatterbox.

"I don't think anyone's allowed to look adorable after thirteen, Lib." I reached behind to unzip the horrid velvet-coloured disgrace to fashion. Libby had insisted on puffy sleeves and A-line skirts. There was absolutely no way I'd allow her to make her four bridesmaids look like something out of Enchanted.

"Nonsense." Libby waved a dismissive hand. "Maybe if you'd shown up to the fitting two weeks ago, we wouldn't be having this argument."

"You're punishing me? Will I be the only one in this dress?"

"God, Danielle. If you're so worried about the extra post-natal fat you've kept on, maybe you should go on the P90X diet. Or maybe Zumba?"

"Excuse me?"

Libby reached out and slapped my hips. "More cushion for the pushin'. Isn't that what they say?"

Now I see why Jules despises you, I thought murderously, tugging the stupid dress off. Humiliation burned through me and I ended up being more violent with the poor dress than was warranted.

"I'm being a friend, Dani," my so-called friend went on, completely oblivious to how badly I wanted to smack her in the teeth. "If you want me to get the dress in a bigger size, I can –"

"No, thanks," I said sweetly. "My fat arse and I are perfectly fine squeezing ourselves out the door."

"Dani, don't be like that."

Ignoring her, I sauntered back into the changing room and pulled my jeans and T-shirt back on. Libby was waiting outside for me, biting her bottom lip.

"Dani? Are you really mad at me?"

"I think you should be mad at yourself for being a total bitch," I replied. "But that's my biased opinion."

"This is childish."

No, this was the best possible way I could get out of attending a wedding I certainly didn't want to attend.

"I might be bigger than you, Libby, but you should know – these hips don't lie."

"Zed is Jazz's son?" asked Jules, now on her fourth chocolate brownie. "And Libby still wants to marry him?"

I laughed bitterly, running a cloth along the countertop to get rid of imaginary crumbs. "Don't even ask me how I found out. Libby certainly wasn't going to tell me, until the wedding dinner where I'd inevitably see my mum and Jazz sitting as parents of the groom."

"Why haven't you ever heard of him? Hasn't Jazz ever talked about her life pre-exit of the closet?"

"Jasmine and I don't sit down for tea and watch EastEnders together while pouring out our hearts to each other," I said sardonically, "so forgive me if I never knew she had a son who just happens to be marrying one of my friends."

"Don't you think you're being a little irrational?" Jules motioned for another brownie. "I mean, God knows how much Libby gets under my skin, but cutting her off just because she's associated with your mother's girlfriend is a little too much, don't you think?"

I placed another brownie on her plate. "She should've at least let me know that her fiancé is Jasmine's son. That's just courtesy. I bet Jasmine's the one who made her keep it some kind of sordid secret." My gaze flickered out the window once again and Jules turned in her seat.

"What is it?"

"Nothing."

She swivelled back. "Try that again."

I gave her a wry smile. "Okay, I'm just being paranoid."

"Understandable," she said furiously. "I know you don't want to hear this again, but honestly, Dani, when I said you need to live a little, I didn't mean go around sleeping with gangsters and getting shot at."

"You're right," I snapped, folding my arms across the front of my dress. "I don't want to hear this again." It had been an utter mistake to confide in Jules. All she'd done was berate me my foolish mistakes and judge me as if her name were Judy or Mathis. The only thing that kept me from bashing her brains out in annoyance was the fact that she agreed that Gavin unassumingly watching Mickey and his babysitter was a great idea.

"All right. I'm sorry," she said gently, stuffing the rest of her pastry into her mouth.

Megan came up beside me, a panicked look on her face. I was struck by a sense of déjà vu.

"What's wrong?" I asked, sighing resignedly. It wasn't Megan's fault that she was always at the wrong place at the wrong time.

"There's someone to see you out back," she hissed, wringing her hands together like an old maid. "He says it's urgent."

Subtlety wasn't Angelo's thing so I didn't have to fear finding him standing at the back of the coffee shop. However, that didn't stop my heart doing the cha-cha against my chest as I gave Jules an apologetic look and turned to head to the back. It was strictly a delivery zone. Only trucks were allowed entry through those gates, yet there was the now familiar BMW parked outside the door leading into the storage room.

Carlo was languidly leaning against one side of the car, his hands shoved into the pockets of his black slacks. He straightened up when I approached him.

"What part of I never want to see you again did you not understand?" I exclaimed, my heart jumping because I'd actually missed that familiar scowl.

Not to mention the sex, my conscience chimed in. You've missed that too bloody much, if you ask me.

"Why didn't you tell me Angie was terrorising you?" Carlo's voice was equally loud and heated.

"Because I figured you knew!"

His brow furrowed even deeper. "How twisted do you think I am? Merda, Danielle! I've punished Angelo for what he did. When will you start to believe that I would never hurt you or Mickey?"

"I stopped believing that bullshít when you had a gunfight in my fúcking house!"

"I was protecting you!"

"I wouldn't need protection if I'd never ever met you!"

I was breathing heavily when I'd finished. Carlo nodded to himself.

"I'm not sorry I met you. Or my son."

"I can't do this corny rubbish," I breathed, turning to leave.

Carlo's hand shot out to grab me. I couldn't have walked away even if I still wanted to. He made me look at him, his hand cupping my chin. I was going to drown in his orbs of green sea if his touch didn't kill me first.

"I don't let people see past my exterior," he said in a low voice, taking my hand in his and pressing my palm against his chest, "but I want to show you that I deserve to be a part of Mickey's life. I'm not asking for your forgiveness, Danielle. I'm asking for your time."

I wished I could erase the mental image of the corpse in my living room. I wished I could overlook Carlo's cousin threatening to kill my son. I wished I could forget what it felt like to have Carlo's body on mine; to have his deep voice in my ear and his calloused hands running along the yielding softness of my skin.

Forgetting all of that was never going to happen. Not in a million years.

"What do you have in mind?" I asked, trembling when his fingers trailed along my spine.

He leaned in and I automatically let my eyes close. When his lips found mine, I threw my arms around his neck and gave him free range with my body. It was suddenly difficult to remember why I'd denied myself the sweet pleasure that was Carlo's mouth.

He took my bottom lip into his mouth, gently sucking on it and eliciting the softest moan from me. He picked me up, his arms supporting my backside, and set me on the hood of his car without tearing his lips from mine. It was a blessing that it was overcast, or the top would've burned me. Even so, I couldn't believe how badly I wanted Carlo. I didn't care if we had sex on the hood of his car as long as we did. My hands searched for his fly and he shook his head.

"No, this is for you – the first in a series of apologies," he growled, pushing me back onto his hood and pulling up the hem of my dress. I was about to protest – and then his hands were caressing my inner thighs.

If anyone – like Megan – came out to see what was taking me so long, I'd have to live down the humiliation for years to come. But I wasn't thinking. Didn't care. His touch was incredible.

"I was thinking," Carlo was saying, his fingers dancing dangerously close to my wet crotch, "you and Mickey could come to Naples with me."

"What?" I breathed.

My panties were next to go, hanging around my ankles. Carlo grabbed my thighs and pulled me towards him, supporting me as he pressed his lips against my innermost flesh. I let out a gasp of pleasure, thrusting my pússy against his mouth, seeking an instant release, a release I wanted so badly I could almost taste it.

But Carlo pulled away. "What do you think, cara mia?" he asked, tasting me on his lips. "Does a vacation sound good?"

"Don't...stop," I pleaded.

"Answer my question."

"Yes, yes, yes!"

A smile tugged at one corner of his lips. "Excellent." And he pressed the pad of his thumb against my clít, gently circling it and making me even needier for him to finish what he'd started.

"Stop," I begged. I was never really good at surviving the torture that was cunnilingus.

Carlo spread the lips of my cúnt with his index finger and thumb, lowering his mouth to my centre. As lightly as he could, he blew cold air against the heat of my sex. I whimpered for him to stop, meaning the opposite, and his tongue slid out and licked its way along the length of my slit. I arched my back and his tongue went in as far as it could go. I moved my hips, wanting him to shove his whole face inside me if that would make me climax, if that would make this torture end.

And then he gripped my thighs as he worked me to a quick orgasm. His hands were hot against my skin and I could only imagine how hot his c0ck would be inside me... That very image brought me to an explosion I couldn't control. Body racked with shudders, I came, biting my bottom lip to keep me from screaming.

"Wow," I exhaled as Carlo kissed my sex one last time and raised his head, the evidence of my release spattered all over his face. He wiped it off with a handkerchief.

I pulled my knickers back up and hopped off his car, shaky on my feet. So Carlo held onto me, and I let him, not wanting to admit how good it felt to be in his arms. Safe.

"How does this weekend sound to you?"

I looked up at him, momentarily confused.

"Naples," he elaborated.

"Oh. That. Lovely, really." I paused. "As long as it'll be just you, me and my son."

He smiled slowly. "Sì, of course."

As he kissed me, I couldn't help thinking how wonderful it would be to not have to worry about Angelo Donafrio for a few days. After all, the real danger was Carlo.

Wolves often wore sheepskin.

Chapter 7

"I'll race you."

"What? No, thanks. I've had a glass of wine and I can't –"

"You can't what? Swim?" Carlo propped himself up on the yellow-brick edge of the pool, most of his body immersed in the enticing azure water. "I can't say that I'm surprised."

"Excuse me?" I said, folding my arms across my chest as I glared down at him. "I am a very good swimmer, thank you very much. Co-captain of my secondary school's swim team, in fact."

"Really?" he smirked. "Tell me this, cara. Why have you spent the past three days gazing wistfully at the water if you were co-captain of a swimming team? Most women would have been naked in my pool the minute they got off the plane."

What had I been thinking about after the almost three-hour plane flight?

Oh yes, that's right: This was a huge mistake.

I'd known that Carlo was a ridiculously wealthy man but it hadn't sunk in until I'd asked which airline we'd be flying with and he'd casually replied, "Airline? No, cara mia, we're taking my jet." I'd spent the entire flight pretending to be extraordinarily engrossed in every little thing Mickey was doing while Carlo deliberately ignored me on his laptop.

"Carlo, I'm sorry I can't be like most women who probably just want to have sex in the pool with you," I said snidely, wondering why I'd even come outside when it was almost midnight and I should have been tucked away nicely in the queen-sized bed upstairs.

To watch him, another voice helpfully put in.

Carlo had the habit of doing the oddest things until the early hours. When he said he was an insomniac, he wasn't joking. The fact that I'd been given the bedroom directly beside his meant that I could hear every noise; every sound. He'd watch old Italian movies on his television, play soft music – if rap could be considered soft or music – go out for a swim or a walk, or sit in silence. It was disconcerting. Whenever his door opened, I'd hold my breath and – idiotically – hope against hope that he'd push my door open. It was unthinkable to even contemplate that I wanted his touch; that after Mickey fell into a content slumber in his cot beside me, I could yearn for Carlo to come and relieve my frustration. I'd had a pep talk with myself the minute we'd arrived at his enormous villa: No sex, Danielle. You should be wary of him. Question his intentions. Question every word that comes out his gifted mouth. Transform into a poetically asexual being.

But I didn't listen to myself.

He hadn't touched me in three days. Three fucking difficult days.

We'd talked – oh, we'd talked far too much – and we'd gone out and that was it. Carlo was intent on showing me the sensational side of Naples. The bay was gorgeous and Mickey enjoyed a few licks of Neapolitan ice-cream. After years of hearing about Mount Vesuvius, it was magical to catch a glimpse of it. The San Carlo Theatre was amazing. Carlo had gotten us the best seats to listen to a man who sounded suspiciously like Pavarotti. We'd eaten out at fancy restaurants. Neapolitan pizza was, quite frankly, the most orgasmic I'd ever tasted. I was slowly starting to understand how my taste buds had been deprived of good food and it was shocking.

That was all well and dandy but, much as I tried to fight it, what I really wanted was Carlo. In every way.

"You don't want to have sex in the pool with me?" asked Carlo, feigning astonishment. "My, how shocking. Water has always been such an aphrodisiac. I need to re-evaluate my life."

"Shut up," I muttered, kicking off my flops. "If you want a race, I'll give you a race."

"Grazie mille," he said, pushing away from the edge into a smooth backstroke.

I tugged my dress over my head, flinging it onto a chaise-longue behind me. I'd bought my bikini at Top Shop the year before and it had become a little constricting around my chest. I was acutely aware that my breasts were practically spilling out as I dove in at the deep end. The water was icy cold, which was an incredible surprise as I knew the pool was heated when the temperature dropped.

Carlo popped up beside me, his hair clinging to his skull endearingly. "Dio mio, Danielle! Is that a swimsuit or a wet dream?" His eyes had decidedly settled on my chest.

I reddened. "What?"

"Now I see why you were so adamant about not swimming," he said quietly, pushing me to the corner without using his hands. "You were afraid I wouldn't be able to control myself."

I was shivering from the cold. At least, that's what I told myself. "It's getting late. I know you don't sleep but I do and...and this wine is extremely potent."

He chuckled. "Relax. I'm going to give you a head start." He swam away from me. "Last one there is a drug lord and mass murderer."

"You're being ridiculous," I said, and launched myself forward.

I could feel him easily slide underwater beside me, but he pulled back, letting me win, and I came up for air, throwing him a dirty look.

"I wasn't aware you were going easy on me," I grumbled. Typical. Men were either letting women win, or sore that they could do it on their own. Adam and Charlie had always been accommodating of my gender disability.

"You were co-captain of your high school's swim team," Carlo said sarcastically. "You won fair and square."

"Cheat." I splashed water into his face and he groaned.

"I just don't know how to please a woman," he said. "You're annoyed that you won?"

"Oh, you definitely know how to please a woman," I blurted out before I could stop my tongue.

"Go on," he persuaded.

I averted my eyes. "That's not what I meant."

He tilted my chin upwards with his hand. "Why have you suddenly become so shy? Is it because you're not comfortable with sharing my home? Or are you thinking about Angelo? Which one is it?"

"I don't know what you mean."

Carlo muttered to himself in quiet Italian. "Do you trust me?"

I didn't open my mouth. We both knew the answer to that one.

His brow furrowed. "What do I have to do to earn your trust? Give you my blood? I've opened up to you; told you things I haven't even told my family. I've invited you into my home. Yet you still don't believe me."

The question I'd been aching to ask was burning on my tongue. Before I could lose my chutzpah, I spat it out.

"How did you get so rich? You said you're an entrepreneur but that's so vague it's almost a lie."

He released me as if he'd been burned. "Do you see all this?" he snarled, gesturing at the house. "I worked for it! I was a street kid; a pickpocket. I worked the fúcking skin off my fúcking bones until I made something of myself. No doors were opened for me and I couldn't pick them. I had to wrench them open myself and I will never forget that. So whatever sordid crime story you've made up in your head? Think of a different plot. I don't need to explain a damn thing to you, or to anyone else, for that matter."

"Are you done?" I asked. "I don't appreciate your raising your voice to me." I reached out for the rail of the steps leading out of the pool.

Carlo snatched my hand in his. "I don't appreciate your questions."

"Wasn't the whole point of this trip for you to convince me that I shouldn't take out a restraining order against you and your psycho family?"

"Mickey is a Donafrio. Don't forget that."

"He's a Clarke. That's what's on his birth certificate and that's how I'm going to raise him."

"Now you're being ridiculous. You know that I want to be a part of his life."

I took a deep breath. "Could you be honest for one second and tell me what you really want with my son? Because I don't buy the doting-father act for all the haggis in Scotland."

His face hardened. "I want to make love to you, for starters. Then I want to make you understand that I'm not the bad guy. But in no particular order."

No sex, Dani Clarke. Asexual...asexual...asex...sex...sex...sex...

"I don't know what's on your agenda for the rest of the night, but I intend to take a shower before slipping into bed for all eternity," I said serenely, turning and going up the steps. "What did you think, that I'd fall into bed with you like some horny teenager?"

"Who said anything about a bed?" he called after me.

"God, did you really make this croissant?" I asked, involuntarily squeezing my eyes shut as I took my final bite.

Ana was standing opposite the table when I opened my eyes again, a wry smile on her face. "Not croissant. Cornetto. Sì. I made it this morning. Good?"

"Excellent," I said truthfully. "You'll have to give me the recipe."

"Better with coffee." Ana reached over and poured me a mug of black coffee.

I put in a spoon of sugar before slugging it down and burning my throat. "Amazing."

"Now I can give Mickey his breakfast?"

Mickey?

Dazed, I turned to look at him in his highchair. He was grimacing at me, obviously annoyed that he was being forced to watch me eat.

"Sorry, tiger. Mummy's being a stingy beast, isn't she?" He didn't seem amused. "Yes, Ana, you can take him into the kitchen. Thanks." She was already scooping him up into her arms. Ana was fifty-seven and her only child had died in a boating accident in his twenties, so she'd never gotten the chance to be a grandmother. It was love at first sight when she laid eyes on Mickey and the feeling was mutual. I wasn't going to deny her the pleasure of feeding him. Out of all Carlo's staff, she was by far the most endearing. The rest – especially the self-righteous security – were highly intimidating and made no attempt to converse in English with me.

"Buongiorno." Carlo's voice came from behind me as he went around the table and took the seat at my right hand. "Sleep well?"

"I slept extremely well, thanks. Did you manage to get any sleep?"

He grimaced. "I can't believe The Cosby Show still shows on TV. There was a marathon."

"And you...watched it?" I asked, unable to envision the sight of him enjoying such a mundane TV show.

"Yes; until I got bored and masturbated," he said sarcastically, reaching for the decanter of coffee. "What do you think?"

"That you got bored and masturbated."

"Very funny. When was the last time you pleasured yourself? I would bet one of my cars that it was last night."

I reddened, suddenly finding my empty plate extraordinarily intriguing. The truth was that I wasn't really in the habit of touching myself. The nuns at the Catholic school my parents had sent me to as a child had instilled in me that touching oneself was akin to slaughtering a nursery of innocent babies. Still, the previous night in the pool – so tantalisingly close to a furious Carlo – had pushed me over the edge of self-restraint. I'd taken that shower – among other things.

God, what if he heard?

"You truly consider yourself hot stuff, don't you?" I asked, reaching for another croissant-or-cornetto. "Like I said, I slept incredibly well."

Carlo's eyes wandered to Mickey's empty chair beside mine. "Where is he?"

"With Ana," I replied, glad for the abrupt change of subject. I watched him drink his coffee. "Don't you think caffeine's a bad idea for a chronic insomniac?"

He arched a brow. "My mother died when I was young. I don't need another one, grazie."

I felt the irritation from the night before come to a boil. "What the hell's your problem?"

"I wasn't aware I had one," he replied coolly, straightening his tie.

"Well, you do, you cúnt!"

"I'm frustrated. Maybe that's my problem, as you put it. You won't let me touch you. You won't let me make you see any kind of sense. What do you want from me?"

"The truth!"

"I'm telling you the goddamn truth!"

"Mr. Entrepreneur? Yeah, right." I rose from my seat. "You can forget about taking me out because I'm certainly not going anywhere with you. In fact, I should be on the next flight home. I have a job, in case you didn't notice, Carlo."

"I'm not keeping you hostage. Feel free to leave whenever the hell you please," he snapped.

"How gracious of you." I marched out the dining room and into the kitchen, where Ana was talking to Mickey in lilting Italian.

"We're leaving," I announced to her, and she quirked a brow.

"Now?"

"Ana, how much do you know about your boss? How much do you really know?"

She reluctantly handed Mickey over. "Is anyone perfect? Dio solo giudicherà – only God will judge," she told me. "Carlo is good to people who need him, even when they do not ask. He creates jobs. Do you know how...generoso that is?"

That was possible. When we were out on the Neapolitan streets, all kinds of people came up to Carlo to greet him, after he'd shooed his bodyguards away, of course. There wasn't a single person terrified of him. In fact, I'd go as far as saying that they worshipped him.

"Ana, questo è sufficiente."

I turned around and found Carlo standing in the doorway. "Funny enough, I actually understood that."

"I go now." Ana slipped past Carlo and left us in the kitchen.

"Don't ever interrogate my staff," Carlo growled, blocking my exit.

"Don't ever tell me what to do. Besides, I wasn't interrogating her." Mickey was squirming in my arms. It took me a second to realise that he was reaching out for Carlo.

"Let me," he said, and I was forced to give my son to him. Mickey was instantly placid, burrowing his nose into Carlo's chest. I swallowed.

"I think I...should go upstairs," I whispered, fighting the urge to burst into uncontrollable tears.

He stepped aside to let me pass and I gratefully slid past him. When I looked back, I caught him nuzzling Mickey's hair. I couldn't deny the fact that he was actually very good with him. Even if he didn't seem like father material, he certainly acted the part.

But it's going to be so difficult to make Mickey forget Carlo when this is all over, I told myself as I blatantly ignored a guard stationed at the foot of the winding staircase and went up to my bedroom.

"What have you gotten yourself into, Dani Clarke?" I asked myself, leaning against the closed door.

What was the real purpose of this trip? To confide in each other? For Carlo to flash his VISA everywhere we went to make up for endangering my son's life and killing someone in my house? For him to be my tour guide? For him to call Mickey his figlio as he blew raspberries onto his tummy and made him giggle?

"Bullshìt," I said aloud.

Carlo was a wolf and wolves always had a hidden agenda. I just had to figure out what the hell it was.

I probably wouldn't have seen the dress if I hadn't made my way past the bed on my way to the bathroom. No male had ever bought me a piece of clothing before, not that I'd expected it, so it was an incredible shock to think that Carlo had had someone choose a dress for me.

It would have been a grand gesture (I'm human, after all) or peace offering if it hadn't so obviously been a wedding dress.

I tentatively picked it up, afraid of damaging it. Made of the thinnest lace and tulle, it was a long-sleeved, floor-length affair that was cinched at the waist. It was gorgeous – old-fashioned but beautiful.

"It's the same design as my grandmother's."

I was sick and bloody tired of Carlo creeping up on me.

"What's the meaning of this?" I asked, not even bothering to turn around. I was afraid to look at his face and know the answer to my question.

"Did you really think I'd let my son grow up a bastard, or worse – raised by the prick you're sure to marry?"

"This is absurd, Carlo," I fumed, practically causing myself whiplash when I spun around to confront him. He was already so close but I wasn't about to be intimidated. "You promised me that –"

"That I what? That I wouldn't pursue custody? I'm not. I'm pursuing you," he barked, making me jump back. "I would never let a child of mine mill about with no identity."

"He has an identity," I screeched, choosing to ignore his blatant attempt to make me lose my will at the sound of his declaration of lust. "He's my son. What happened with the Healey Group or clinic or whatever wasn't my fault! Sue them and be done with it, but don't you dare... Carlo, stop it."

He was getting on bended knee and I was momentarily astounded, more than ever when he produced a ring.

"Stop!" I hissed, as if someone were watching.

"Danielle Clarke, we might not love each other, but we have a common goal – to protect Mickey," he was saying, his eyes so intense I could almost believe the words spewing out of his mouth. Almost. "I can offer you protection, security – the moon. Perhaps lust can evolve into love, cara mia."

"Lust can evolve? Listen to yourself!"

He frowned. "It took me a while to come up with that one."

"Good job. You're one line away from a modern-day Shakespeare. Now, if you'll excuse me, I should –"

"Merda, Danielle," he cursed. "I stopped begging when I was a boy. You can't possibly want me to start now." He punctuated his sentence by getting to his feet and, with one hand moving to the back of my head, claimed my mouth with his.

There was no way I could lie and say I didn't want to kiss him.

The dress fell to the carpet as I draped my arms around his neck, parting my lips for his tongue to duel with mine. His hands were on my shoulders, pulling down the thin straps of my dress. I shimmied out of it while he shrugged out of his suit jacket. Without warning, he pushed me back onto the bed and positioned himself over me.

"Close your eyes," he whispered into my ear, his lips lightly grazing my earlobe.

I did, and was instantly bombarded by a fleet of questions by my conscience: Aren't you supposed to be telling him to go to hell? That marrying an alleged gangster isn't on your bucket list? Why won't you think about your son? What will people say about you? What about Angelo?

I was about to voice my complete and utter refusal to be his bride for convenience's sake when I felt him raise my arms and cuff my wrists to the bedpost above my head. My eyes flew open.

"What the hell?"

"Relax," Carlo said soothingly from between my legs, his hand lightly caressing my inner thigh. "I knew I'd need to convince you, bella mia." He leaned down and placed a soft kiss so close to my already wet crotch before slipping my knickers off.

I was supposed to fight, wasn't I? To pull away from the iron-wrought bedpost; to kick at him?

But I didn't.

I was intrigued.

Jules was one of those kinky types; the ones that let their boyfriends smack them and call them dirty slags. BDSM just hadn't been my cup of tea, so it was fascinating to wonder what Carlo was going to do to me. He started by reaching under the bed for what turned out to be rope and then producing a blindfold from his pocket and effectively turning the morning into night.

"This is how you plan to convince me to marry you? You must be delusional." I experienced a brief moment of panic. We hadn't discussed any rules, any safe words, any likes and dislikes – nothing. And yet...I did trust Carlo.

He didn't say a thing, grabbing my right ankle and tying it to the other end of the bed before binding my other leg. The rope bit into my skin but I didn't complain. In fact, I was beginning to like it.

And then just like that, he disappeared out of the bedroom, the door audibly closing behind him.

"Carlo?"

Silence.

"You prick!"

I finally squirmed, only making the rope dig even deeper into my skin. Wincing, I bit my bottom lip to keep myself from screaming.

Marry you? I'm going to murder you! I thought viciously.

It was probably only minutes but it felt like hours until I heard the door open.

"I'm going to kill you," I said in a low voice, although I knew I wasn't in a position to be making any threats, spread-eagled and tied up.

There was an interminable silence until I heard him move. And then I felt it – cold and utterly foreign – between my breasts.

"Gelato," Carlo whispered, and his mouth came down to remove it. "Chocolate gelato."

His mouth was warm in contrast to the ice-cream. He was slow with his tongue as he ran it down the valley between my breasts, drawing out a soft moan from me and I quivered, wishing I could see. He used one hand to unsnap my bra from the front and tear it off completely. My breasts were aching, begging for his attention.

But he drenched my quivering belly in ice-cream.

His tongue was hard as a sword against my stomach and it flickered out almost frantically. I arched my back, only serving to make the rope sink even deeper into my ankles.

"Do you want me to be gentle, bella mia?" Carlo's mouth was travelling lower. "Or perhaps you want me to be as violent as you think I am?"

I couldn't talk; couldn't breathe when his tongue was so close to where I wanted it to be.

I felt him withdraw. Breathing heavily, I nearly wanted to shout – until he took my nipples in his hands. They were hard and erect, and when he pinched them, I gasped in surprise. I felt his mouth suddenly draw one in; licking it, sucking it, nipping it, until I lost my scruples and screamed in delight.

"Marry me," he breathed into my breasts, squeezing them against his head.

"No," I gasped, and as I'd expected, he withdrew from me again.

I listened for him and heard nothing for a long time – until I felt his fingers on my swollen clìt. He wasn't applying much pressure and that was more agonising than if he'd rubbed at it with gusto. He was torturing me. Even so, I began to rotate my hips as best as I could under such duress, telling him that I wanted that.

"I bet you want me to slide myself inside you," he said softly, so soft he could've been a completely different person. "You want me to spread you apart and enter you. Gently? No. With such force that you're afraid I've maimed you for life, sì. You want me to penetrate you further than I've ever gone, lo so." His fingers were now teasing my inner thigh.

"Yes," I hissed, knowing that my cúnt was dripping and that the only thing that could satisfy me was Carlo Donafrio.

"Sposami," he breathed. "Marry me."

"We...can't..." I panted, nearly coming when I felt his tongue on my opening.

His breath was so hot, so torturous that I was finding it difficult to form a coherent sentence. Slowly, he licked the bottom of my lips, tasting me. He licked his way up, his tongue wide and flat against my slit. My hips moved of their own accord, and my breathing became shallow as I anticipated what came next.

He pulled away and I fought with the handcuffs, trying to get free so that I could strangle him.

"I know you can't see me," he said, his voice suddenly in my ear, "so I'll paint a picture for you. You're wet, but I think that was a given." His mouth was on my neck. "You're so ready for me, as I am for you, but I want to make you suffer." He sucked on my flesh. "The thing is, I'm good at self-control, but not with you. Not with you, Dani cara. I get aroused when you're angry." His teeth grazed my skin and I let out a wail. "I get aroused when you're happy. Dio mio, I get turned on when I watch you breastfeed – did you know that?" His hands sought a nipple and found it, teasing it between two fingers. "There's something about your breasts, so heavy with milk and desire, that could drive me insane with hunger. I only want to make you happy."

I am going to come, I thought, biting my bottom lip.

"So I ask again – will you marry me?"

"Don't," I whispered, when his hand strayed down my belly and into the folds of my cúnt. I shuddered with a mini orgasm, biting my bottom lip to keep from screaming.

"Yes, or no?"

Two fingers slipped inside me, seeking my core. I arched my back and whimpered.

"Please!" I begged softly. "I want your c0ck. I want it so badly I can hardly think!"

He retracted his hands and I waited impatiently.

But of course, Carlo had his own plans. I felt him move all the way up among the pillows and then, after a beat, felt what I knew was his hardness against my cheek. Pre-cum instantly dripped down my neck and I did the only thing I wanted to – I turned my head and opened my mouth.

Carlo eased himself inside and I drew him in even further. He released a guttural moan when I began to suck him. I was becoming even wetter. The fact that I couldn't see – only hear and feel – made giving him a blowjob all the more arousing. He was slowly moving his c0ck around inside my mouth, in no hurry to climax. I could feel his head brush against the back of my throat and stretch my mouth, so huge it was a sin.

If it was possible, he was becoming harder, my tongue able to feel the veins on his shaft become more apparent. I clamped down even tighter when he suddenly grabbed my hair with both hands and, groaning, murmured, "Enough."

My mouth opened and he withdrew, his breathing laboured.

"Be mine, Danielle," he said fiercely, and this time, I changed my answer.

"I will."

And I felt his c0ck against my opening, rubbing against my clìt before he drives himself into me in one plunge. Keeping most of his weight off me, I could still feel that he was completely nude. He was vicious in his thrusts and the handcuffs and ropes ensured that the pain was maximised and that only heightened the orgàsm I had. Carlo continued to thrust into me, gripping the sheets with each one. I came again and again, until finally, he climaxed as well, his cry muffled by my neck.

My blindfold was removed and I was face-to-face with Carlo, his nose only a breath away. He placed a kiss on my nose before pulling out and rolling onto his side beside me. Reaching out, he removed one of my hairpins and, without much fuss, unlocked my cuffs.

My wrists were rubbed raw and I sat up, stroking them. Carlo sat up as well, taking my hands in his.

"The fact that you let me tie you up shows that you do, in fact, trust me," he said quietly, lifting my wrists to his lips to be kissed in turn. "I could've taken our son while you lay here naked and bound."

I thought about it. "Trust has to be earned and your hoodwinking me into coming here to engage in a marriage of convenience is far from charming, Carlo Donafrio."

I pulled my hands away and got to work undoing the knotted rope at my ankles. Carlo removed them in seconds.

"I did not hoodwink you," he said, tracing the curve of my spine with one finger.

I turned to look at him. "I won't be coerced into something I don't want. This is going to be on my terms, okay?"

"Sì," he said, a smile tugging at his lips.

"I'm serious!"

"I know."

"Good." In one clean manoeuvre, I got onto his lap, straddling him. Carlo's hands snaked around my waist to steady me. "Mickey comes first. Always." I brushed aside a stray lock of his curly hair.

"I know," he said intensely.

"And I'd love to visit Capri for the day. You know, for our honeymoon?"

"You'll love it." He smiled.

I leaned down. "Did you really mean what you said? About my breasts basically making you horny?"

He cupped my left breast in one big hand and squeezed. "What do you think, Dani cara?"

Chapter 8

It was stupid to feel this way but I did.

You can't be a wife, Dani. It's not in your DNA. That's the real reason you can't settle down.

Carlo thought my aversion to marriage was because it was to him, but it was more than that. Marriages were like Pyrex dishes – they always broke, no matter how hard you tried to ensure that they didn't. This particular marriage, on the other hand, was going to end. It wasn't real. It wasn't real and it shouldn't have mattered but somehow, it did.

"What am I doing?" I asked myself, squeezing the bouquet of gardenias in my hand so tightly that they wilted.

It seemed like the aisle was the length of the Great Wall of China. Of course, it very nearly was. The chapel Carlo had picked out was near the Teatro and overlooked the busy harbour. It had been built in the eighteenth century by several faceless men and commissioned by a king who was just as unimportant, yet it was one of the most beautiful buildings I'd ever seen.

"What's the point of a church?" I'd asked Carlo when he'd told me where the ceremony would take place. "You don't even believe in God."

He had scowled at me. "Even if this is a marriage of convenience, we are going to do it right, Danielle. My nonna would never have accepted a casual stroll to the court." His voice became reverent whenever he mentioned his late grandmother and I couldn't help but find that sweet.

In an alternate universe, I might've been jittery. I might've tried on the wedding dress and loudly criticised my body while Ana brushed my harsh words off and told me how gorgeous I looked. I might've wondered what the groom would be thinking as I glided down the aisle, if he was as nervous as I was. I might've worried that my mum would bring Jasmine as her plus one and further humiliate my father. I might've worried about the food, the seating arrangements, the wedding song and whether Mickey would be overwhelmed by all the lights and get too excitable.

I wasn't thinking of any of those things. I couldn't have cared less about the stupid dress, although I was the first to admit that it was certainly tasteful. As it was, Carlo's unreadable poker face only served to make me weary as I neared him at the altar. I didn't have to fret over any wedding guests because Ana, Mickey and Carlo's bodyguard, a man called Rio, were the only witnesses to our sham of a wedding. They sat in the first pew of the otherwise empty chapel.

"Try to relax," Carlo said in my ear as soon as I took my place beside him. His hand was on the small of my back in a move that was supposed to be comforting. It wasn't.

"I can't," I told him, "because I can't help but feel that I was coerced into this." Even as I said it, I knew I was lying. Being with Carlo was the only real way Mickey and I could be safe. It was convenient. It was logical.

"I did not coerce you," he said in a low growl. "I asked you, and you said yes."

The priest cleared his throat, signalling us to shut up. He looked like a holier-than-thou version of Father Christmas, with his portly belly visible in his robes and his curly silver hair. Half-moon glasses were even perched on his nose before bright, hazel eyes. Carlo had told me that he'd asked the Father to speed the Catholic ceremony up and it was obvious the priest was more than happy to do so.

"May we begin?" he asked, his Neapolitan accent far heavier than Carlo's.

"Sì," Carlo swiftly affirmed, glancing at me.

"Whatever," I offered.

If Father Russo was astonished by my less-than-ecstatic answer, he did a brilliant job of not showing it. Instead, he cleared his throat again and began to read something about the holy matrimony being a pillar of honesty, love and trust. I instantly zoned out, my eyes settling on the wall behind the altar. Intricate paintings depicting famous biblical events took up the entire space. Art had been one of my favourite subjects at school and I vaguely remembered studying the Renaissance artists, like Botticelli, Michelangelo and Pinturicchio. This looked like some of their work and it was utterly compelling – so compelling, in fact, that I didn't realise Father Russo was looking at me expectantly, the heavy silence indicating that he'd been doing so for a long time.

"Sorry, what?" I asked.

From beside me, Carlo muttered something under his breath. It was probably a curse. He shouldn't have been cursing in a church.

"Your vows?" Father Russo patiently prompted me.

"Forget them," Carlo snapped. "Just ask her if she takes me."

"Do you, Danielle Clarke, take Carlo Donafrio as your lawful husband, to have and to –"

"I do," I interjected, matching Carlo's boorish eagerness to get this mess over with.

"But I have not finished," the Father protested, giving us a puzzled look in turn.

"E'bene," said Carlo, all but snatching my hand and putting the ring on my finger.

"I must bless the ring, Signore Donafrio." Father Russo's voice was barely more than a wheeze.

Carlo ignored him, sliding his own ring onto his finger.

"How romantic," I said dryly, flexing my hand before me. I couldn't deny that, just like the dress, the ring was stunning and probably cost a fortune, judging from its carat-size estimate. It sparkled in the dim light of the church, a beacon in an otherwise murky storm.

Without warning, Carlo's hands were on the back of my head and we were kissing. My eyes immediately shut and I turned boneless, my lips parting on a sigh. Kissing Carlo was like going to the casino – you never knew what to expect but you easily became addicted. I was powerless to resist him. I didn't want to. His tongue flickered past into my mouth with the promise of more, tasting me; exploring me, until my oral nerve-endings felt like they were enflamed. And just like that, he stopped and pulled back. My eyes fluttered open and, embarrassed, I looked away.

"Grazie mille, Padre," Carlo thanked the priest.

"Er... prego. Bless you and go in peace."

Carlo's hand swallowed mine. "See? That wasn't so bad, was it, Signora Donafrio?"

He was right. It was worse than I'd imagined because a small, microscopic part of me was a bit disappointed that we weren't marrying for love.

"And has he taken his bath? Lukewarm water, remember?"

"Sì. He has had his bath."

"Make sure you check on him every hour, even when he doesn't make any noise. He might seem okay but he's different and –"

"Signora, I had a child, you remember?" Ana interjected through the phone. "I raised him alone, like you."

I bit my bottom lip, pressing the phone even closer to my ear as I glanced at the closed bathroom door of the hotel room. "I'm sorry, Ana." I sighed, leaning back into the pillows. "It's just that...we're so far away from you right now and I've never been this far from Mickey before. He might not know what to make of it."

Ana let out a soft laugh. "We are on the next island, Signora, not on another continent. Please, enjoy your honeymoon. I go now."

"OK. Goodnight. Give Mickey a big kiss from me."

"I will." She hung up and I was left holding the telephone and contemplating phoning her back.

"Cosa fai?"

I hadn't noticed Carlo coming out of the bathroom, a towel wrapped around his waist and his hair dripping. Sitting back up, I slammed the phone back into its cradle. "You know, being married to you doesn't mean I suddenly come with Google Translate."

"Funny," he said, in a voice that told me he didn't find me even remotely amusing. "I was wondering what you were doing but it was quite obvious. Checking up on Michael?"

"You can't blame me. What sort of mother would I be if I didn't?"

He padded over to the vanity table, his back to me. "Then why did you look incredibly guilty, cara?"

"Because... because you're making me feel that way." I got off the bed and pulled my suitcase open, rooting inside to locate my toilet bag.

"You're the one that wanted to visit Capri."

I did. After hearing about it in university from a friend who'd stayed at the Capri resort with a boyfriend, I'd only dreamed of saving up and going there myself. Located on the south coast of Naples, Capri is one of the most romantic paradises known to man and I had been dying to experience it myself.

"I know, but I didn't realise I'd have to leave my son."

"Ana is a very capable minder. I trust her. She has fallen in love with our son." His voice was surprisingly soothing and it dissolved all my worries.

"Maybe, but Mickey's...different. You know this."

His brow furrowed. "You mean the fact that he's not really walking or talking? Perhaps a trip to the doc-"

I cut him off right there. "My dad didn't start talking or walking until his fourth birthday. His parents didn't take him to the doctor to be told some rubbish about him being mentally slow," I said through gritted teeth. I sighed. "We shouldn't have left him, Carlo."

"Call me selfish but I wanted you to myself."

I flushed, burned by his heated stare. "I should...go."

Snatching my bag, I hightailed it to the bathroom, closing the door behind me.

"Call me selfish but I want you to myself," I mumbled to myself, setting my bag on the sink. "Does he really expect me to buy that cheesiness?"

I shimmied out of my petticoat and grabbed my shampoo. Now completely nude, I pulled open the mottled-glass door and simultaneously turned on the hot and cold water, letting it steam the place up. My stomach rumbled and I sighed, placing my shampoo on the soap ledge. My appetite had waxed since the beginning of the trip but for the first time in a long time, I didn't give a damn. Food was meant to be enjoyed and no dipshit called Libby Wilson was going to tell me otherwise. The last time I'd eaten was on the one-hour ferry ride from the Molo Beverello port to Capri, far too distant a time for my body to remember.

"Mm," I murmured when I stepped under the jet of water. Showers were better than bubble baths any day.

But a bubble bath with Carlo would certainly hit the spot.

As if possessed, my hand wandered below my abdomen. Even at such and advanced age I thought touching oneself wasn't quite right. That still didn't stop me from rubbing my clìt. It was remarkable to discover that one simple mental picture of taking a bath with a man could get me so hot, so wet. I didn't realise how ferocious I was in my quest for an orgasm until I came, mewing as I held onto one wall for support.

The door was pulled open and Carlo stood there in all his naked glory, putting me to shame.

"I was... I wasn't..." My voice trailed off because an explanation wasn't necessary. It was painfully evident that I was masturbating on our honeymoon.

"You don't have to do that," he murmured, stepping into the stall and closing the door behind him. "You don't have to do that when I'm here," he said more forcefully.

I took a step back, my back hitting the wall. The shower suddenly didn't seem as huge as I'd thought it was a minute. "I wasn't satisfied anyway."

"Naturalmente," he said huskily. "What will satisfy you?"

That was easy.

"You."

He was less than a breath away. "Then turn around and let me satisfy you."

I turned.

Carlo's arms snaked around my waist, firmly pulling me to him while I pressed my palms flat against the wall. His erection was pushed against my tailbone and it took all my willpower not to beg him to give it to me right then. Instead of focusing on my already wet cúnt, Carlo's big hands came up beneath my tits and cupped them. Despite the heat of the water raining from above us, my nipples stood erect, making my arousal tangible. Slowly, the pads of his thumbs began to circle the hard nubs. They were painfully hard and the pain became unbearable when he tweaked them between his fingers, torturing me.

"Stop," I moaned, reaching behind me with one hand and grabbing his c0ck.

He groaned, jerking. "Don't." His hands left my breasts.

"I can't wait," I said impatiently. "I want you now."

I felt his mouth on the side of my neck and my breathing became erratic. "You turn me on when you say such things," he whispered, his tongue running down my skin.

His hands were unhurriedly dancing down my tummy, my skin taut and wet. Just the feel of him encompassing me was enough to make me so close. I wanted to feel him everywhere; in every orifice, every pore. I didn't care how; I just wanted him.

When he finally parted the folds of my cúnt, I bit my bottom lip in anticipation, hardly able to stand. The difference between my fingers and his was amazing. For starters, his were much bigger than mine, thus more satisfying. He played with my pulsing clìt, making me shudder in his hand on the brink of yet another climax. Slowly, he slid a finger inside me, testing the waters, before sliding another. I clenched myself around his fingers, arching my back as he worked a rhythm. With his free hand, he massaged the water into one of my breasts, cupping it and making me gasp for air. His mouth on my neck and his hardness pushed against my back, Carlo's hands were what really made me come. I came violently, a mass of whimpers and gasps. I screamed louder than was normal and he held me against him, quelling my spasms.

I turned around and he enveloped me in his arms, his head dipping for our mouths to meet. His hand cupped the back of my head as he deepened the kiss. I wanted him completely and irrevocably and, sensing that, he raised me, his arms coming up under my rear as I wrapped my legs around his waist.

Water pelting my back, I looped my arms around his neck and he entered me in one fluid thrust, pushing me up against the wall. With one hand, I held onto the ledge for support, knocking my shampoo and shower gel off. I clenched myself around his c0ck, and Carlo groaned in response, the sound shooting straight to my clít. He thrust into me again, further than before, deeper, and I bit down on his bottom lip in happy surprise, drawing blood.

"Carlo," I gasped, my fingernails biting into the taut muscles of his back. "Deeper. Deeper."

He drove into me again and again, and I thought I'd explode. I rode him in a more than lithe way, finding his rhythm as he increased it with his need. In a massive explosion of cries, I came, feeling Carlo throb inside me as I clamped around him. Stars burst behind my closed eyelids and then Carlo was emptying himself inside me sporadically, nearly squeezing the life out of me before pressing his face into my breasts.

I ran my hands through his wet mop of hair until he raised his head and our eyes met.

"Let me wash your back, cara mia," he said softly, pulling out before setting me down on the ground.

I could barely stand on my own two feet. Carlo bent to scoop up the shower gel, squirting it onto his hands. I turn my face to the shower head, squeezing my eyes shut. At his vigorous touch, I felt myself begin to get aroused once again. He worked the soap into lather on my shoulders, then my back and rear. His hands soaped my breasts, sensitising my nipples again as he rubbed in circular motions. I leaned back into him as he spent an unusual amount of time making sure my chest was lathered enough. Carlo definitely was a tits man.

He eventually moved to my stomach, my muscles instantly tensing from the sensation.

If I'd thought it couldn't get any agonising, I was completely mistaken. He worked his hands between my thighs and I stopped him before I exploded once more.

He turned me around and cupped my chin, drawing in for another kiss. I could get lost in his mouth and I could feel that I already was – irrevocably and completely lost.

"I'm getting pruned," I protested when he pressed my palm against his sudden hardness.

He chuckled, releasing me so I could rinse off. "Indeed."

"You're insatiable."

"You're addictive."

I laughed. "Stop it."

Leaving the shower stall was like coming out of a steamy alternate universe. Carlo handed me a fluffy, white Hers towel with the Hotel Marina Grande insignia proudly running along one edge. I took a smaller one and wrapped it around my head turban-style before rubbing myself dry and binding the towel around me under my armpits. I remembered that I hadn't washed my hair and wrinkled my nose.

Oh well. There's always tomorrow morning, I thought to myself, watching Carlo leave the bathroom. His shoulder blades were peppered with red bruises from where I'd maimed him with my claws and I couldn't bring myself to feel remorse.

I wiped the steam off the mirror and saw how red and swollen my lips were. I fingered them with an index finger before tilting my head and running a hand down the right side of my purpling neck. I closed my eyes, the memory of his tongue on my neck imprinted on my brain. How could I ever have thought I'd be able to resist him? Why would I want to?

Have you forgotten, you stupid trollop? He's dangerous, enigmatic and is related to the nutter who threatened your son.

"Yes, but he's also sweet – sometimes – and cares about Mickey," I said aloud, removing the towel around my head and allowing my hair to fall to my shoulders.

I left the bathroom before my conscience replied and damned me to hell.

Carlo was still in his towel when I sauntered into the bedroom, sitting on the edge of the bed with his mobile in hand. He looked up when I came in.

"Restaurant or room service?" he asked, putting his BlackBerry down.

I cocked my head. "Room service." I removed my towel and let it fall to the carpet. "If that's okay with you, caro?"

Carlo's gaze became predatory. "Exactly what I was thinking."

"Did you see those fish?" I asked incredulously, after pulling off my snorkel and throwing it onto the russet-brown sand. With great difficulty, the rest of the equipment came off.

Romeo, our baby-faced scuba-diving instructor, came up behind me to unzip my wetsuit before bending to pick up the rest of the gear. "Beautiful, no?"

Beautiful didn't even come close to it. The closest to any large expanse of water for me was a visit to the Isle of Wight with my gran when my brothers and I were younger. It had rained cats and dogs and we'd stayed inside playing Battleship until boredom drove my brothers to play-fighting.

"Bella!" I exclaimed instead, squealing when Carlo unexpectedly picked me up from behind.

"Are you really flirting with this kid in front of me?" he asked, setting me back on the ground.

I turned around and threw my arms around his neck. "Flirting? But I only have eyes for you, Signor Donafrio."

"Do you now?" His eyes had darkened to a colour I recognised as arousal. "I bet you say that to all the men on the beach."

I got on my tiptoes and kissed the man who passionately refused to wear a wetsuit because he insisted that he would look like a fool, but wasn't ashamed to show his scarred chest in public. He kissed me back with a fiercer passion, his lips scalding mine with a heat more intense than the sun beating down on my back. I could still taste the metallic bruise on his bottom lip where I'd bitten him the night before. He tasted divine and I didn't care that we were giving the other tourists sunbathing on the Marina Piccola beach a show.

With the luminescent horizon and glimmering blue water as our background, I could see why Sian, my friend from uni, hadn't wanted to leave.

Carlo pulled back, biting his lower lip. "Andiamo," he said gruffly.

"Where to?" I asked, although I had a pretty good idea when I felt the bulge in the front of his board shorts.

His eyes glittered. "Back to our suite. Where I will continue to make love to you until you can only speak Italian."

"Sí," I told him. "Sí a thousand times."

"Did you know that this beach is said to be the spot where Odysseus almost succumbed to the Sirens' alluring song?" he said, his hand cupping my chin.

"Do you believe in legends?"

His eyes seemed distant for a second. "I believe that all legends have a pinch of truth to them, bella mia." He returned his gaze to me. "What I do know is that I am not as strong as Odysseus was...because, unlike him, I have surrendered to an English rose of a siren."

I felt heat enflame my cheeks. "I bet you say that to all the women on the beach."

"No," he said soberly, "only to the one and only Signora Carlo Donafrio."

Chapter 9

"Are you going to be moving the entire gang into our neighbour-hood?" a raspy voice asked from behind me.

I pushed open my front door, kicked my suitcase inside and readjusted Mickey on my hip before I turned around and fixed my nosy-old-hag of a neighbour, Mrs. Walters, with a puzzled stare. She was standing on my doorstep, nearly a foot shorter than me.

"What?" I immediately wanted to heave when the smell of wet feline wafted into my nostrils. Lillian Walters was the proverbial cat lady. On a good day, the sound of her fifteen tabbies purring and yowling next door could only be heard when I opened the living room windows.

She dug into her tatty, khaki shoulder bag and handed me a well-thumbed magazine. "I'm disappointed in you, Danielle. I thought you'd marry a nice, sensible young man."

I snatched the mag from her, keeping it out of Mickey's eager reach. There were a number of things that went through my mind at the sight of MOBSTER MARRIES HIS MAIDEN splashed across the celebrity section – like how the hell Glitz had managed to follow us to Naples – but my main concern was that if batty old Mrs. Walters had seen it, chances were that my family had, too. I dreaded checking my mobile.

"Don't you have a life?" I asked venomously, nearly flinging the thing back at her.

"I beg your pardon?" Her watery eyes widened in disbelief.

I used my hand to block Mickey's ears. "Get the fúck off my property. Clear enough for you?"

"I hope your mother's proud of you, cursing like a sailor," she muttered, slowly turning to shuffle off my porch.

I watched her go, breathing heavily. She had no idea how close I was to committing murder. A movement by my garage caught my eye and I instantly darted inside, slamming the door shut behind me.

"Mummy?" Mickey sounded concerned. His tiny fingers pulled at my hair in an attempt to get my attention.

I padded into the living room, still clutching him, and peeked through the window. The sight of what was obviously a trespassing paparazzo met my eyes. He was currently peeping into my Fiat. I was boiling with frustrated rage.

"It's okay, baby. It'll be okay," I said gently, juggling him on my hip uncomfortably. I brushed aside a lock of curly hair. "Mum's going to take care of this."

She'll just have to suck up her bloody pride, I thought furiously.

Carlo had wanted me to stay at his penthouse and this had turned into an ugly argument when I'd refused point blank. He'd compromised by having Gav follow me home and again, like a complete loon, I'd said no. Well, I wasn't going to dwell on my stupidity but how was I supposed to know that there'd be photographers sneaking through my gate?

"Mum's going to take care of this." Maybe if I kept mumbling this mantra enough, I'd believe it.

Mickey didn't seem to believe it either. I knelt down and propped him up on the carpet, digging into my shoulder bag for his favourite teddy and handing it to him. He promptly began to make Teddy climb all over him.

"Think, Dani, think," I whispered to myself, peeking through the curtains once more.

My driveway was empty now, save for the car. Gav popped up from the blue, noticed me, and nodded.

I dug into my pockets and pulled out my phone, punching in a number I really shouldn't have known by heart.

He answered on the first ring.

"Is everything all right, bella?"

"No!" I hated it when my voice became high-pitched. "Everything is not all right and do you know why?"

He heaved out a breath. "Gavin just notified me of the unfortunate peeping Tom. He was disposed of."

"And have you seen the papers?"

"One tabloid does not constitute as the papers," Carlo replied calmly, his cool tone only succeeding in irking me.

"What am I supposed to do? Hide inside until they lose interest?"

"Perhaps if you'd listened to me – your husband – and accepted my reasonable offer of accommodation..."

That shut me up.

"Dani?"

"I'm thinking. Look, you might be used to this, but I'm not," I said, biting my bottom lip.

"Gavin is parked outside. Should you wish to change your mind –"

"We both know I have."

"Good. I'll see you soon, cara."

I hung up just in time for the door to be barged open and for my brothers to burst inside in a highly unnecessary fashion. Any hope of dodging them until I made up an explanation for the paps and tabloids and my elopement was quickly extinguished.

"Dani!" Adam barked.

"Danielle!" Charlie seconded.

"In here," I called back, resigned to my fate.

"There's a skinhead outside who says he's your bodyguard," Charlie said in disbelief as Adam pushed past him and went to his nephew, who was eagerly raising his arms to be picked up and got exactly what he wanted.

"Do you want to give Dad a heart attack?"

"What possessed you, Dani?"

"Did he threaten you?"

"I'm gonna kill that cúnt!"

"We're going to kill him."

"Would you both shut up?" I screeched, silencing them. I took a step back. "Did one of you eat garlic?"

They raised their brows.

"I had some garlic bread, yeah," said Charlie. He shook his head. "Nice try at changing the subject, sis. We're not gonna –"

"You reek," I groaned, and pushed past them, dashing up the stairs until I got to my bathroom.

I knelt before the toilet bowl and promptly upchucked the last of Ana's meals.

"You okay?"

I looked up, angrier than anything. "You and Adam can stop worrying about me and get the hell out," I spat, shakily getting to my feet.

Charlie folded his arms across his chest, the sleeves of his T-shirt straining. "Nice rock," he remarked, his eyes zoning in on my finger. "Did he pay for that with drug money or prostitution cash?"

"Go away and stop talking." I bent over the sink and splashed my face with cold water before grabbing a spare toothbrush and running it over my teeth. It wasn't enough. I needed Listerine.

"You wish. Dani, you might be older than me by – what? – two minutes, but I'm not going to stop looking out for you. I don't know what Donafrio has on you but –"

"He's the best shag I've ever had," I interjected, only because I wanted to get rid of my brother. I spun around just in time to catch the look of derision on Charlie's face. "That's right, Charlie. I've slept with him. And let me tell you, once you've had a taste of Italian sausage, you can never go back to English rashers."

Charlie looked as nauseous as I felt.

"Are you okay, Charlie love? You look a bit pale."

"This isn't over," he said through clenched teeth.

My stomach lurched. "I'll walk you out."

"Just tell them to get the hell out, Meg." I paused, waiting for her whining in my ear to end. "Yes, yes, I know you can't physically force them to leave but you can call the police." Pause. "Two words: No comment. I know, I know, and I'm sorry." Pause. "Maybe tomorrow. Depending on how I feel. No, it's not serious. Just a bug, I think. No, I haven't been kidnapped. Look, I've got to go. Thank you so much."

I switched my mobile off as soon as the call ended. My brothers had left me a dozen messages, my parents had left me four each, and Jules and another handful of girlfriends had left me hundreds. Apparently, eloping was just plain rude.

Megan, on the other hand, was frantically trying to keep reporters out of the café and while I sympathised, I couldn't be bothered to worry about that right now. I had far too much to deal with.

"He's asleep."

Carlo's deep voice startled me and I pivoted to meet his eye. He was leaning against the doorjamb, his hands in the pockets of his black basketball shorts, looking completely edible. I rarely saw him out of his suits – unless he was naked, which, when I thought about it, was most of the time – and I decided I preferred him less imposing. I could imagine Mickey nuzzling into Carlo's bare chest just as easily as I could imagine myself in his arms.

Stop that, you weak little slag.

What's the matter? He is my husband. I have every right to perve over him.

Yes, and probably fall for him in the process like an idiot.

"That was fast," I told him, secretly disappointed because Mickey had kept me occupied and now, fast asleep, had left me alone with his father.

My inner voice was right. Back in Italy, I could pretend that everything was normal, that we were just an average couple on holiday, but in reality, there was nothing normal about holidaying with my sperm donor who just happened to be under investigation for murder, among other things.

"I'm good with kids," Carlo said offhandedly, coming into the room and closing the door behind him.

Just like that, I was claustrophobic. It was ridiculous, as Carlo's massive bedroom was far from being a confined space. Like him, it was fascinating – the walls were a stark-white, wacky paintings providing a break from the neutral colour, a chandelier casting the most intense light hung from above the king-sized four-poster, and ridiculously plush garnet-coloured carpet running beneath my bare feet. This was my first time in Carlo's penthouse and it was blatantly obvious that this bachelor pad wasn't child-friendly. There was far too much glass and expensive things.

"I won't be able to deal with people following me around, asking about you," I said quietly, taking a step back and nearly tripping over my newly-packed suitcase. "When do you think it's going to stop?"

A shadow crossed his face. "No one is going to follow you, bella mia. No one is going to interrupt your life."

"You're not God."

"Sì, but that doesn't mean I can't protect you."

I hadn't noticed how close he'd gotten until he tipped my chin upwards. "Are you okay?" he queried, his eyes searching mine.

"How can I be? I want to go home but I can't because I'm being stalked. I want to get back to work but I can't because I'm being stalked. I want to
–"

His lips met mine and the rest of my complaint died in my throat. I didn't get how he could do that – make me forget what was important; make me think he was the only thing that mattered at that particular moment. It boggled the mind.

His hands gripped the back of my head, his fingers threading my hair. He tasted of...garlic.

I pulled back, breathing heavily. "I can't."

Carlo's eyes went skyward. "What is it?" His probing gaze returned to me. "Do you know what that ring on your finger means?"

I knew that I was always going to reflexively look at my ring whenever anyone mentioned it. I did right then.

"It means that you're mine, Dani cara. All mine."

"It's not that," I breathed, and I dove past him and all but ran into the bathroom. I didn't bother to close the door but this time, the queasiness didn't give way to a retching spell.

I squeezed my eyes shut and counted to ten. With Mickey, it had been cinnamon. This time, it was garlic. I could smell it everywhere, even now, in the bathroom where the stench of garlic couldn't possibly linger.

I bet you're having a right laugh, God. I wish I could share the joke.

"Something I said?" Carlo's sarcastic voice came from behind me.

"More like something you did," I muttered under my breath, counting to ten again in my head. "Something you did again and again and again."

"Fifteen pregnancy tests, Danielle. These are the things I do for you," Jules said for the tenth time that morning, finally removing her oversized sunglasses and propping them on her head. "The girl at the counter probably thought I was a loon. Why don't you just go to your doctor if you want to be especially sure?"

I shook my head emphatically. "I can't. What if she tells?" Although Dr. Gordon had delivered Mickey ad knew the truth about his conception, there was no way in hell I'd go to her clinic during this time. My pregnancy hitting the gossip columns would be the icing on the cake and I'd never be able to live it down, not to mention the flak I'd receive from my family.

Still, Jules had accepted my request to go to the pharmacy on my behalf and had, for the past three hours, waited for each and every test to show me just how much I despised the colour pink.

"Ever heard of doctor-patient confidentiality?" Jules said practically, leaning back into the sofa. "Shìt, what is this? Velvet?" She ran her hands along the armrest. "Sure as hell feels like it!"

I'd lost count of how many times I'd rolled my eyes at Jules' childlike amazement at everything in Carlo's house. Jules was supposed to be sophisticated, at least that was the image she painted for the outside world. Deep inside, she was still that girl from Bradford with a dream and the gift of the gab.

"Jules, focus, please?" I tightened my gown around me, feeling as gross as I probably looked. The only real thing I was grateful for was that my stomach had stopped acting up and that Mickey was taking a nap in the next room. "I can't do this again. I'm not ready and this is the worst possible time, worst possible man."

"Oh, come off it, Dani," Jules said, giving me a look. "That worst possible man is now your husband. I know I was doubtful about you and...Carlo Donafrio at the beginning, but don't you think it's Fate having a laugh at you? Think about it: Mickey and this baby will have the same father. I should've been invited to the wedding."

Fate wasn't funny, if that was the case. My hands automatically went to my stomach.

"Carlo's baby," I whispered, testing the words on my lips. I tasted bile. "Do I tell him?"

"Why the hell not? You're married and he obviously likes kids."

But I could think of a dozen reasons not to. For starters, I hadn't planned any of this. I hadn't planned to fall for Carlo, I hadn't planned to marry him, I hadn't planned on moving in with him, and I sure as hell hadn't planned on getting pregnant with his second child. There were many problems with it.

Hadn't planned to fall for Carlo? my inner voice repeated incredulously. What are you thinking?

Panicked, I jumped to my feet. "You should go."

"What, you're not allowed to have any visitors?" she asked, not budging an inch. She shot me a sober look. "Dani, you'd tell me if this was something sinister, right? You'd tell me if you're here against your will?"

"Don't be so melodramatic," I hissed. "I just don't want him to find you here and don't look at me like that. I had to prod Gav into letting you in. Apparently security is a big issue here."

"Yeah, fine, whatever. Just...don't ignore my calls again, you bìtch."

I smiled. "I won't."

"Oh, before I forget – Charlie and Adam are livid. Charlie's exact words, I believe, were I'm not afraid of no immigrant," said Jules. "Very PC, your brother. And his grammar's the best."

"Charlie's never been politically correct," I muttered in disgust. "Would you tell him to calm down? He's making a big deal out of nothing. Besides, Carlo can kick his arse in his sleep."

"What do you expect, Dani? No one knew you and Donafrio were dating, let alone that you'd eloped. Then it hits the papers and we all look like the biggest fools."

"We didn't elope. It just...happened."

"I'm not judging you, okay? I'm being a friend. You have to think practically – for Mickey's sake and now for this baby's."

I swallowed. "Goodbye, Jules."

After seeing her to the door, I checked on my son then took the longest shower ever. By the time I got out the bathroom, it was lunchtime and, feeling slightly refreshed, I went into Carlo's wardrobe and rooted inside until I found an old football T-shirt. His cologne – which I'd long ago identified as Guess – crept into my nostrils and I breathed it in with a sigh of shameless pleasure.

"My, my, my, Signora Donafrio. I didn't know you were a Red Devil," came a voice from behind me. "Then again, that's exactly what you are – a devil."

I bit back a scream when I spun around and saw who it was. Even if I hadn't seen him, I would've recognised that heavily sardonic voice.

"Get the hell out."

"You look well," Angelo commented, his eyes raking over me. "Then again, money and a tan will do that to a person."

"I'll scream," I told him. "I'll scream and Carlo's guards will come in."

"I'm family, you puttana." He kicked the door closed behind him, the sound echoing in the quiet penthouse. "You know, I have to congratulate you. You're not Carlo's type – not even close – yet you managed to get him down the aisle. What'd you do, promise unlimited access to your bastard son?"

Anger seized me. "Listen, you dìckhead, the next thing that comes out that filthy mouth of yours should be an apology, or so help me, I will kill you," I hissed, balling my hands into fists.

"You wouldn't even be here if I hadn't been stupid enough to go looking for you, bìtch," Angelo snapped in response, approaching me. I stood my ground. "You wanna know something incredibly hilarious?" he snarled. "The hospital actually contacted Carlo about his magical sperm. Asked if they could use it. I was dumb enough to say yeah, sure, why the hell not? Make an inadequate woman happy. What kind of incompetent hospital doesn't confirm who they're speaking to?" His brow furrowed. "My cousin's going to be in for a huge motherfúcking shock when that hospital argues that he let them use his cum. Funny, huh?"

"You're mental. And pathetic. Don't you have a life?"

Angelo scowled at me. He was so close I could see the vein in his forehead pulsing. "You just don't get it, you thick wh0re! I was next in line. I was going to be rich. And now where's all the money gonna go when Carlo croaks? I'll tell you – your precious little bastard son!"

"I...I don't know what to say..."

"Then don't say anything!"

"You didn't let me finish, you sick fúck," I said through gritted teeth, stepping toward him until we were practically eye level. "I don't know what to say, except that if you ever think of harming my precious little son, you won't see another day. I don't give a damn about the Donafrio empire, whatever it's based on, so you don't have to worry your empty head about that. And one more thing: I wonder what my husband would think of your threats – because this time, I'm going to tell him."

He glared at me. I glared back. The door was pushed open.

Angelo jumped a mile and my breathing returned to normal. Sort of.

"Am I interrupting something?" Carlo asked coolly, setting his briefcase on the ground.

"I was just leaving," said Angelo, moving to sidestep his cousin, who blocked his exit.

"What are you doing in my bedroom?" Carlo's voice was nothing more than a growl.

"Carlo, I –"

"I continue giving you chances to redeem yourself but time after time, you prove to be an idiota. Did I not explicitly tell you to stay away from Danielle?"

"I was congratulating her. You know, the wedding?"

"Actually, what he was doing was calling my son a bastard," I said, shivering when Carlo's intense eyes swivelled to meet mine. "You should know that your cousin is hoping to take over...whatever it is that you do when you die."

"Angie, come with me," Carlo said in a low voice. "Don't look at me like that." He changed tack – probably to shut me out with the language barrier – and started speaking rapid Italian.

They walked out together, and Carlo slammed the door shut behind them.

Without preamble, I went to pick up Carlo's briefcase and snapped it open, setting it on the bed.

"Entrepreneur, huh?" I said to myself, rifling through the stack of papers. Most of the documents were of the legal variety – Donafrio vs. The Healey Group – but I didn't stop until I found something interesting, which turned out to be after a long while.

Paranoia kept me glancing at the closed door. I was utterly horrible for snooping but what else was I supposed to do when Carlo wouldn't tell me the truth about himself? I had to know who I was married to.

There were other copies of ridiculously official papers, mostly lawsuits against Carlo. The newspaper article about the murdered club owner sprang to mind when I saw an assault charge against Carlo. Johnson, David claimed that Carlo had sacked him for stealing from one of his nightclubs but had gone as far as attacking him to teach him a lesson he'd never forget. He had lawsuits from Earth to Neptune.

Carlo, apparently, owned nightclubs from here in our little old town to New York, Paris, Milan, Athens – the list was endless. He owned restaurants – Italian pizzerias, French bistros – and this very block of luxury apartments, among others. Nothing too shady, I was forced to admit.

So maybe he's telling the truth, Dani. Close the case and go see if Mickey's awake.

But I saw my name and couldn't resist looking.

True to his word, he'd had me 'checked out'. It was strange to see my entire life reduced to a folder – my photos, my medical information, my financial information, hell, even my weight...everything. In fact, my whole family was in there, even Jazz.

I kept thinking I'd find a bag of coke, or pictures of prostitutes but I came up empty.

"What are you doing?"

Guilty, I whirled around, dropping the pages back onto the bed.

"I shouldn't have invaded your privacy," I murmured, hurriedly shoving his documents back inside the briefcase.

"Just give me that," he snapped, grabbing it from me.

"What happened to...to your knuckles?" I asked, although I already knew. I had two brothers. I'd seen my fair share of red, raw fists.

Carlo didn't answer. He had every right to be pissed off.

"Can you blame me?" I asked meekly, watching him go into the bathroom. My stomach growled. "Shut up," I hissed at it.

"I could've killed him," Carlo said, leaving the bathroom. He'd undone his shirt and I suddenly felt incredibly aroused, which was an understatement. I could've jumped him then and there, relishing in either angry or make-up sex. "Why are you looking at me like that? Find anything interesting in my private things?"

I reddened. "I'm sorry. It's just that –"

"You don't trust me."

"I do. I wouldn't have married you otherwise."

"Don't insult my intelligence by lying, Danielle."

I'm pregnant. Again. Do you want a baby? Another one?

But I couldn't make my mouth and brain co-operate to say those words.

"Is Mickey your heir?" I asked, pushing the thought of telling Carlo out of my mind. "I mean, if anything happens to you, have you put him in your will?"

A smile tugged at one corner of his mouth. "Are you thinking of joining forces with my cousin and having me murdered?"

The idea horrified me. "What? God, no! I'm just...curious."

He unconsciously rubbed his knuckles. "Don't be."

"Yes. Fine. I'm hungry."

Carlo stepped before me. "I'm sorry Angelo said those things to you. You'll never have to see him again."

"It's what he said about my son that –"

"Our son," Carlo corrected, and I could have melted when his arms slipped around my waist. "I should be at a lunch meeting," he said huskily, "but Dani, I don't think I can stay away from you."

"I'm sorry," I repeated. "I do trust you. You make me feel safe and...I need that." I got on my tiptoes and kissed him lightly. "Carlo, I need you. Now."

He dipped his head and mashed his lips against mine, walking me backwards until the back of my legs hit the bed and I fell back. He kept the bulk of his weight off me, one hand sliding up my bare thighs and immediately discovering that I was going commando.

"Are you still mad at me?" I whispered, releasing a mew when his fingers played with my opening.

"I was never mad."

"Oh, but I want you to be."

He looked at me. "What?"

"I want to have the angriest sex ever," I replied, and he smirked, pulling back.

"Then in that case, cara mia, you've just pissed me the hell off," he growled, ripping my T-shirt – his shirt – into two.

Food could definitely wait.

Chapter 10

"A drink, sir?"

Her name was Goldie – at least, I thought it was. Hanging over me, her breasts in my face and the faint smell of her sweat and over-compensating perfume assaulting my nostrils, she couldn't have been more obvious.

"What are you wearing, signorina?" I asked, tapping my fingertips on the armrest of what Angie had called the Throne. It had been a present at the club opening from Don Romano, the go-to guy for every kind of furniture under the sun. The Throne, in particular, was one of his best creations. With a high back and golden, velvety exterior, it was aptly named and, because I rarely sat in it, was in pristine condition. I noticed things like texture and design. Coming from such an underprivileged background, it was too damn hard not to, even now, when money was no object.

Goldie – or whatever her name was – glanced down at her front. "You mean my top? But...Gio said cream is just like white, only...more interesting. Should I...change?"

"What does the sign on the building say?"

"Eleganza?"

"And what does that mean?"

"Elegance?"

"Sì. Do you really think that – with your breasts on show like a common puttana – you are anything close to elegant?"

She bit her bottom lip and shook her head.

"Signorina, I run a respectable business," I informed her. "If you want to dress like that, there are plenty of seedy nightclubs for the picking and you are free to leave whenever you so desire. Understood?"

"Yes."

"Good. I'll have a whisky, no ice."

She all but scampered away like a hunted rabbit.

"Should you really be drinking in the morning, mio fratello?" Gio called out, approaching me with a bottle of Heineken in his hand, the hypocrite.

"Fatt'i cazzi tuoi," I muttered, accepting Goldie's proffered glass. She was fast, I'd give her that.

"Unfortunately, I can't mind my own business," Gio replied in English, taking a long swig of beer before sitting on the divan opposite me. "What are you even doing here? You know I've got this Eleganza under control. What, you're running away from the signora?"

I regarded him with a glare over my glass. If Gio were anyone else, I would have punched him for his insolence. As it was, Giovanni Bianchi was Mia's baby brother and the closest thing to a confidant and brother that I had. Five years my junior, I trusted his judgment more than I did that of my own blood. Angelo had more than proven that water could be thickened if need be.

Fúcking stupido.

"Seems a little quiet today," I remarked, downing the JD in one gulp and placing the glass on the table.

"Day being the operative word. Business is at night." Gio arched a brow. "Everything all right?"

I gave him a wry smile. "Are you playing the diary to my Bridget Jones?"

"I knew you were an undercover pússy," said Gio, setting his empty bottle on the glass table. "Come on. Try me. Problems with the wife? Problems with the law? Both?"

"I don't care about the law," I told him with a snort of disgust. "They're just running in circles. No concrete evidence – nothing. I'm just glad my next hearing is two months away. Marino will get me acquitted. Again."

"Oh, yeah? Good, good. Fúck this town, though. If we were back in New York, you'd have been scot free a long time ago." Gio paused. "So I guess it's your woman. Man, I never figured you for a family guy. I thought you loved your bachelor lifestyle."

"I have a son."

Gio blinked at me, silence filling the air. "So that's why you had the shotgun wedding," he said after a beat. "You knocked her up. Cristo, Donafrio – ever heard of protection? What the hell happened to you?"

I bit back a retort. Uno...due...tre...quattro...cinque... Making it to five without lashing out was always a surprise.

"I did not...knock her up. Michael's three."

"Then I don't understand."

"Don't try to," I muttered. Mia – sweet Mia who had only wanted to birth a Donafrio – still had no idea that the child that had been intended for her was another woman's. I wouldn't break her heart by telling her and Gio would never lie to his sister, no matter how strong our bond was. I valued his loyalty too much to ask him.

"Does he look like you?"

An image of Michael popped into my head. It was fascinating to realise that I had committed every eyelash, every dimple to memory. Family came first to me and Michael was mine. He had my eyes, my hair. He had my blood coursing through his veins and one day, he'd call me his father. I could hear the sound of his throaty laugh; feel the way his tiny fingers pulled at my hair, and inhale the scent of talcum powder whenever he snuggled with me when he was sleepy. At thirty, I knew for certain that billions of pounds, Euros, dollars – whatever – could not amount to a child saying that one word – papà.

"You'll meet him," I replied, and the look on Gio's face told me that I probably looked like a dreamy idiota. I cleared my throat, rising. "I should get going. I have a meeting with Marino in an hour."

Gio followed suit. "When will I meet her?"

Mai, I thought fiercely. It was irrational to think that; to never want Gio to meet Danielle. He was family. She was family. Why the…jealousy?

Jealousy was inaccurate. It bordered on downright barbaric mistrust. I had noticed it growing over the past week Danielle had been in my house. I continuously thought about what she was doing, who she was doing it with – and the jealousy grew with each passing day. It pissed me off. I had never behaved in such a juvenile manner. Besides, I had nothing to fear. Danielle preferred to hide out at home, claiming she couldn't face anyone until she was ready.

"Her life is being turned upside down. Chi sa?" I shrugged. "I'll let you know. Ciao."

"Ciao," Gio said, looking at me strangely.

Before I could leave, Goldie – if that was indeed her name – advanced upon me. She'd discarded the unfortunate top and had opted for a more tasteful blouse. I mentally commended her improvisation.

"What is it?" I snapped, in no mood to converse with the barmaid.

She took a step back and I inwardly sighed.

"Scusa. I'm in a rush," I said, softening my tone. The only woman who had ever ordered me to never raise my voice at her was Danielle. Danielle had a backbone.

"Sorry, sir. I just...well, I just wanted to thank you," Goldie murmured, wringing her hands together. "I'm glad you didn't look at my tits."

"You're not my type."

I stepped around her and walked out, annoyed. How dare a staff member talk to me in such a manner? I was going to have to speak to Gio about that, but first, my lawyer and I were going to have a very lengthy discussion.

"I couldn't stop them," Gavin explained quickly, getting into the elevator with me. "I apologise, but I just couldn't stop the lot of them."

"Don't. Speak."

Silence filled the lift until it dinged to a stop outside my door. Gavin made the smart move of retreating to a far corner in the lift, allowing me to leave. What did I pay security for if they let any Tom, Dick and Harry saunter onto my floor?

They were in my living room and Danielle was standing in the centre, crying. Danielle wasn't supposed to be crying. I couldn't bear to see cara mia cry; it was a physical pain, something that caught me off guard.

"What did you do to her?" I asked the man I recognised as her father. I'd seen a picture of him before and I never forgot a face.

He was old, but not as old as my own bastard of a father had been when he'd appeared in my life six years ago, wanting money. No, Michael Clarke was far younger than my mother's first love had been.

"Carlo, don't," Dani said softly, hugging herself protectively. She must have assumed that I'd attack her old man in a heartbeat – and I would have, if he admitted to causing her pain.

Michael Clarke was silent, though, and looked as if he were completely out of it. This was one of the few times I regretted my decision to draw the line at household staff. I had no clue about entertaining guests in such a personal setting. It made me...uncomfortable.

"Mr. Donafrio?"

I tore my gaze away from him and finally noticed the two women occupying the other sofa. One of them had the same chestnut-coloured hair as Dani, although greying slightly, and the other looked to be about as tall as me.

"Mrs. Clarke?"

She rose to her feet. "Yes, hi. But actually, I'm not married anymore."

"Piacere di conoscerla," I said, taking her hand. "It is a pleasure to meet you." My eyes travelled to the woman beside her. "And I assume that you are her sister?"

She smiled, and Danielle snorted from behind me.

"No, I'm her partner, Jasmine."

Of course. The hippie.

"Carlo doesn't want to hear about that." Danielle grabbed my arm and tugged me towards her. The electricity that shot through my arm at her touch could have powered a small village. "Could I speak to you, caro?" she hissed, and, although she couldn't have pulled me even if she tried, I allowed her the notion that she was indeed doing so.

"What's the matter?" I asked once we were in our bedroom. "Of course, I meant to talk to your parents at some point. I'm not an ogre, Danielle. If they –"

She shook her head. "It's not that. Well, yes, they're obviously annoyed, especially given your reputation, and don't get me started about my brothers...but..."

"But what?" I cupped her face in my hands. Danielle's skin was the softest I'd ever felt. I didn't want to think of kissing that skin just that moment.

"My dad remarried," she whispered, and the tears started all over again.

She buried her face in my chest, her arms snaking around my back. I pulled her into me, kissing the top of her head.

"Isn't that good news, bella?"

"No," she whimpered. "God, I'm so infantile. I kept hoping my parents would get back together and now...now there's no hope."

"Is she half his age?" Perhaps that was the real problem. Dani would certainly never accept a stepmother her age.

She choked out a laugh into my chest. "It's my doctor, Elizabeth Gordon. She's perfectly legal." I recognised the name. According to Mickey's medicals, she was his doctor. "They got married the same day we did. How ironic. My useless brothers didn't even bother to tell me. Am I that pathetic?" She pulled away from me and sat at the foot of our bed. "I'm trying to stop weeping like a baby but everything's going wrong," she wailed. "My dad remarrying, this pregnancy, the whole publicity thing... I just... I want it all to stop, Carlo."

I looked at her. "Scusi? What did you just say?"

Dani blinked at me like a deer caught in the headlights. "Oh crap." She let out a heavy sigh. "I didn't want to tell you like this. Clearly your sperm transcends the power of contraception." She let out a laugh that turned into a sob.

I was frozen to the spot.

Dio mio, ancora?

It explained her bouts of arousal – Dani had been insatiable in bed every day of that week – and uncontrollable temper. It all came down to hormones.

"Well?" she said impatiently, her big, liquid, hazel eyes imploring me. "Say something, dammit!"

I cleared my throat and went to her, crouching at her feet. Was she really worried about my response? Was she worried that two children would be too much for a man like me? Just looking into her anxious eyes, I knew the answer and hated it.

"I realise that I have made the most unforgivable mistake, Danielle," I began, gently prising her knees apart as I tried to find the right words.

Her eyes clouded over. "Oh, have you?" Her voice could have cut into rock. "Well, I'm not sorry about this mistake. I might not be so overjoyed right now, but I will love this baby even if you don't want yet another complication in your extraordinarily perfect life, Carlo Donafrio. Just remember that I was fine before I met you and I'll be just as peachy when you leave me."

"Are you finished?"

Dani was breathing heavily after her sudden outburst. If she knew how erotic it was to watch the rise and fall of her chest so close to my face, she would have certainly slapped me. Or, even more likely, undressed me. She was confusing that way.

"Because you didn't let me finish," I continued, stroking the firmness of her thighs through the fabric of her sweatpants. "Why would you think I wouldn't want a baby with you? Another one," I amended quickly. "Dani Donafrio, ti amo. I love you so much that I'm willing to look past your unfamiliarity with the NBA; I love you so much that I would gladly have a soccer team of kids with you; and I love you so much that I'm willing to ignore the fact that you have never said those words to me before. The most unforgivable mistake I have made is not telling you this the minute I laid eyes on you."

Bene, Donafrio. Didn't it feel good to get that off your chest?

Dani's eyes were wide with shock. I didn't blame her. I was amazed the words had left my mouth, too.

"What...what happened to lust?" she wanted to know, wringing her hands. "Remember that? What you said on our joke of a wedding day?"

I deserved that.

"I've never been in love before," I confessed. "Dani, don't look at me like that. It's the truth."

She reached out to touch my cheek. "I would never have stayed if I didn't love you." She paused. "I lied. I wasn't okay before I met you. Yes, you piss me off a great deal, but I wouldn't have it any other way, Carlo Donafrio."

"I...piss you off?"

She laughed, wiping away the remnants of her tears. "Yes."

"But you have to admit, the make-up sex is worth it, no?"

Dani's laugh was like a song. "We're going to have a baby," she said breathlessly.

I took her hand in mine, kissing her upturned palm. I heard her breath catch in her throat and was gratified by how instantly she responded to my touch.

"My parents...they're outside," she whispered, her eyes never leaving mine as I rose to my feet.

"Ssh...non parlano," I told her, ignoring the constant vibration of my phone in my pocket. "Let me do all the talking."

She leaned back onto the bed and propped herself up on her elbows. "I'm listening." She let out a gasp of surprise when I pulled her vest up, cold air hitting her belly, the belly that was carrying my seed.

"Madre dei miei figli," I whispered, placing myself between her legs. I pressed my lips against her navel. "You're the mother of my children," I translated, "and I will do anything to make you happy."

"Ti amo," she breathed out, running her hands through my hair.

I smiled into her belly. "You're sexy when you speak Italian."

"Oh God, Charlie?" Dani shrieked, making me straighten up. Why the hell was she calling her brother's name when we were about to make love?

I followed her gaze to the door.

Charlie Clarke. Of course. He was standing in the doorway with a look on his face that I was quite familiar with. Plenty of men had looked at me that way – the look of a man who was baying for Donafrio blood.

"While you're in here...doing whatever it is that you're doing, your son is bawling his brains out and our parents are out there twiddling their thumbs waiting for you," he said, glaring at his sister. They looked nothing alike.

"Oh God." Dani righted her top before getting up. "Couldn't you knock?"

"Aren't you going to introduce us?"

"Carlo, this is Charlie, my twin. Charlie, Carlo." She gave her brother a warning look. "Carlo is my husband and that isn't going to change. I don't care what you and Adam think because I love him and he loves Mickey and me right back. It's my life and I'll live it the way I want to." She pushed past her brother. "Play nice, boys."

"I love your sister," I pronounced, once Danielle had left the room. I removed my tie, discarding it on the bed. The imprint of Dani's body was still on the bedding. "You have nothing to fear."

"I don't, huh?" Charlie folded his arms across his chest. "So what are you scared of, mate? Why the need for so much security?"

The fact that he was standing in my bedroom was proof that my security level was extremely low.

Let's just get this attack over with, I thought to myself, resigned.

"It's no secret that I have enemies."

"Well, guess what. Your enemies become Dani's enemies. I'm not about to let her put herself in danger for a... Holy shìt, is that you and...Kobe?"

I glanced at the framed photo beside the bookshelf. Gio had insisted that personal pictures added "a certain pizzazz". I hadn't had the heart to dissuade him from decorating my room. "You a Lakers fan?"

"Rugby and basketball – that's my shìt," Charlie replied, going up to the shelf. "When was this?"

"I don't remember. I'm a Knicks man myself."

"But you pose for pics Kobe? I guess you were star-struck."

"I don't pose and fawning over celebrities is beneath me," I muttered, repulsed by the idea, "but the next time I visit LA, you should come with me."

He turned to look at me, his blue eyes narrowing. "You're not pulling my fúcking leg?"

Despite myself, I felt a smile form on my face. "I'm not pulling your fúcking leg."

He grinned. "Let's talk details, brother-in-law."

"Don't be ridiculous, Carlo," she breathed into my ear, wrapping her bare legs around my waist. "Of course you won't hurt the baby. Now, get on with it."

I still wasn't convinced that in the throes of pleasure, I wouldn't either fúck too hard and crush the baby, or fúck too hard and hit the womb – but Dani was more knowledgeable about this than I. "Sì," I obliged, beginning to explore her skin. "Whatever you desire."

Her breasts, so heavy and desirable, were calling out to me in a language I knew well. Arching her back, Dani offered me the hard, caramel nipples of her breasts. Each time I tasted her skin, it felt like the first time. Moaning, she grabbed my hair by the roots, pushing her breasts into my face. I held onto her, sucking on her as if she were my air supply.

"Enough," she hissed, slapping my hand away when I traced it between her thighs. "I'm wet and I need you inside me."

I was already hard. I had been hard the entire day. It had been torture during dinner with her parents, watching her eat and feigning disinterest, ignoring my hard-on. Every time she opened her mouth, I couldn't help but behave like a small boy and imagine her mouth closing around my erection. It had made conversation agonisingly difficult and her family probably didn't know what to make about my monosyllabic answers to their probing questions.

"Certo," I told Dani, placing a kiss on her nose. I placed a palm flat against her stomach. "Sei mio. You're mine."

Her eyes were playful. "Should I tattoo Property of Carlo on my tummy?"

"I won't lie – the gesture would be appreciated," I replied, lowering my head and kissing her. Her lips parted and allowed my tongue entry.

Groaning, I entered her second mouth, the force driving her to dig her fingernails into my back. She was beautiful like this, her hair spread across the pillow and her face an animation of pleasure. Dani wasn't one to lie back and let me do all the work. No, making love to her was like having a heated debate with two victors. She met me thrust for thrust, finding my rhythm and driving me that much closer to climax.

"I'm coming," Dani hissed into my ear, her opening clenching around my c0ck. "Don't stop!"

She came, her grip on me rivalling that of a boa. I wanted to make her climax again; make her lose herself in the primal throes of ecstasy as we became one. She did – again and again – until finally, spent, she drew back. I emptied myself inside her, her name the only thing to escape my lips.

"Ti amo," she said, and I knew that I would never get tired of hearing her say those two words.

"I love you, too, cara."

Marino's idea of a "post-nup" arrangement could go to hell. I was never letting Danielle Clarke slip through my fingers.

Chapter 11

"You're going to be okay delivering all those cakes?" I asked Meg for the billionth time, giving her my full attention and simultaneously closing the cash register. I'd been on my feet for hours because – with the sudden fame that came with marrying a billionaire – business was booming. Meg and Catherine, another girl I'd had to hire, couldn't handle that many customers alone.

Meg rolled her eyes at me, giving me a mock salute. "Yes, ma'am."

"I know, I know." I let out a sigh, running a hand through my hair. "It's just that I'm not used to being so... useless."

"You're not useless," Meg said sweetly, "but I do have to deliver that order so...I'll see you later?"

"Yes." I smacked my forehead, remembering something. "You can take the van home. I'll close up."

Truthfully, I was glad to be rid of Megan for the day. The girl just made no sense behind the register. Numerous patrons had complained that she either short-changed them, or gave them far too much.

"Just sack her and be done with it," Jules was fond of saying, especially after the instance when Meg had given her a twenty-pound note in exchange for a fiver.

I wasn't going to be mean. Meg was a sweet girl, despite her irritating and daily commentary: "Why are you still working? Your husband's loaded,

Dani! And God, why do you even stay in this town? Why does he? It makes no sense!"

Clarke's Café was my business. There was no way in hell I'd quit doing the one thing I was good at just because Carlo was wealthy and I didn't need to work anymore. Sure, it felt amazingly refreshing when the 'FINAL NOTICE' letters had stopped coming in the post and when I finally realised that I'd never have to worry about putting Mickey through school – but that was where it ended. Money wasn't the reason I was with Carlo Donafrio. It had been a month since he'd said those amazing words and I never got tired of hearing them because honestly, they – and the way he made me feel – were the reason I was with him. Besides all that, this small town was my home and I could never leave my brothers. At least, that was how I felt right then.

"Glad I could catch you!"

I had completely zoned out and probably had the dopiest look on my face thinking about Carlo. So I had to blink a few times before I could register Jazz standing at the counter, her hair pulled into a massive and ridiculously messy bun and a wide smile on her lined face.

"Jazz. Hello." I tried to force some cheer into my voice, I really did. Despite this, I still sounded like Wall-E.

Ignoring my monotone, Jazz sat on one of the stools at the counter. "I brought you something," she said, rooting into her handbag. "Are you feeling peaky? Craving things?"

"I –"

"This is a cinnamon-and-mint powder. Really calming stuff," she told me, cutting me off. She handed me a Ziploc bag of something horrid that looked suspiciously like marijuana. "You just pop it into warm water and add half a teaspoon of sugar."

"Er, thanks?" I set it on the shelf beneath the till, mentally reminding myself to chuck it away at a later date. I wasn't going to put it past Jazz to try to poison me and my baby.

You're being a bitch, my conscience let me know, and I flushed with guilt. Jazz wasn't so bad. She really wasn't.

"You're welcome." She grinned. "How are things? Where's Michael?"

"Fine. He has a nanny now and we think he's making progress."

I'd expected to be jealous of the easy way Mickey had fallen in love with Theresa – a bright, English-speaking Neapolitan girl who was distantly related to Ana – but I wasn't. She was excellent with him and he was becoming more articulate with his words, even stringing sentences together, sentences he'd seemed to already know. That was the best part of it. She had taken it upon herself to make Mickey speak – both English and Italian – and it was working.

"Any chance he'll visit us?"

"Not anytime soon."

Jazz's face fell. "You're still irked about Zachariah, aren't you? About my not telling you about him?"

"What? I'm way past that, Jazz. I couldn't give two hoots about Zed."

"Could we talk? I mean, if you're not too busy right now?" She glanced around the room. Only three people sat at a table, talking in hushed tones. "I'll take a seat over there, at that table. Is that OK?"

I nodded. "Sure."

She sashayed off, trying to delicately perch herself on the tiny chair and wait for me to join her.

Could this day get any worse? I thought to myself. Bonding with my mother's girlfriend when yet another busy day was coming to an end was far from the top of my list of exciting things to do. Sighing, I walked around the counter and shuffled to her table and reluctantly sat opposite her.

I could do this. I was a grown woman and I could build a fúcking bridge and get the hell over it.

"Libby's been asking about you," was Jazz's opening line when I'd finally settled myself in the chair. "The wedding's been pushed up. She'd really love for you to come."

"I think it's ridiculous for you and Mum to pretend you've never been with men before; to live in some sort of little bubble of lesbian bliss while we outsiders are meant to deal with all the pain you've caused us."

Jazz's mouth became a thin line.

"Sorry," I told her, absolutely mortified. Where had that come from? "Can we just blame that incredibly homophobic statement on hormones?" I pleaded.

"If you let Fiona and I babysit sometime," Jazz said gently. She let out a sigh. "Danielle, I've only ever wanted to be your friend. I've never wanted to come between you and Fiona – ever. If you gave me a chance, you'd see that."

"Okay," I said after a long while. "You can babysit. I'm not going to let Mickey miss out on his gran." I huffed out a breath. "Why did you hide the fact that you have a son?"

"I didn't hide anything. You just never asked."

I couldn't argue there. I hadn't been interested in anything to do with Jazz Lewis and it just wasn't fair of me to be mad at her for adding another family member to my already-confusing family tree.

"Were you in love with his father?" It was an unbelievably personal question but I was dead curious.

To Jazz's credit, she barely batted an eyelash. "No. Unlike your mother, I've always known which team I bat for."

For some reason, that struck me as side-splitting. I let out a laugh, tried to muffle it with a hand, and Jazz's face broke into a smile.

"But I don't regret it, Danielle. Zachariah and Fiona are the best things that ever happened to me," she continued, her eyes conveying her sincerity. "I don't regret having him and I don't regret falling in love with your mother."

"Good," I said softly, reaching out for her hands. She clasped mine, her bear hands swallowing them up. "I didn't exactly hate you because you're female. I hated you because I felt you broke my family up."

Fiona's eyes widened. "I... Fiona thought you weren't okay with her being gay. It never... Well, it never crossed my mind that –"

"It's okay," I told her, squeezing her hands in mine. "My parents weren't happy together and I was too young to see that. It doesn't matter anymore. My mum's happy with you and now, my dad's OK, too."

Jazz gave me a wide smile and a moment of understanding passed between us. We'd never paint each other's toenails but at least we could have a decent conversation. I looked up from her suddenly and saw Carlo standing at the door. Our eyes locked and just like that, it was just the two of us – three, if you were counting our baby inside me.

"Jazz, I have to go," I said, my eyes finally swivelling back to Jasmine.

She turned to look over her shoulder. "Ah. Of course." Grinning, she rose and I followed suit. "Thanks again, Danielle. It was lovely talking to you."

"Same here."

I watched her swan away and receive a chaste peck on the cheek from Carlo on her way out the café. She was almost as tall as him, something that was incredibly scary, considering his staggering height.

"When will you stop this nonsense, Danielle?" This was Carlo's daily greeting as he approached me.

"What nonsense?" And that was my daily answer.

He cupped my face in his hands and swooped in for the kill, wrapping his arms around my waist. Our lips locked and I let out a sigh of pleasure. That was what I'd been craving the entire day.

"You should taste today's special," I told him once he broke the kiss. "It's an old family recipe."

Carlo's brow knitted. "You shouldn't be on your feet the whole day, cara. You'll exhaust yourself."

"I'm three months pregnant, Carlo, not handicapped."

He let out a defeated sigh. "Is it a cake?"

"Yep," I declared, taking his hand. "Your birthday cake."

He let out a groan. "I thought we had this conversation, bella mia. I don't _"

I put my finger to his lips, shutting him up. "Have you noticed something?"

"No," he said softly, his tongue flickering out to lick my finger.

I trembled. "The café's empty." The last of my customers had trickled out, leaving empty crockery on their tables.

I stepped away from him and went to the door, peeking outside. Carlo's BMW was parked by the kerb and Gav was discreetly patrolling the street. I flipped the OPEN sign around, locked the door and went around pulling down the blinds. Finally, I turned to face my husband.

"Happy birthday, Carlo."

He shook his head, a cloud passing over his face. "I clearly recall telling you that I don't celebrate my birthday."

"Come on, sweetheart," I told him, undoing the cloth apron that was straining around my waist. "Thirty-one isn't even old." I discarded the apron on a chair and went to the counter. "Stop being such a female."

"That isn't the reason," he said curtly, following me.

I didn't press for an explanation. Mia – who'd turned out not to be as cold as I'd initially thought – had told me that Carlo never explained his eccentricities to anyone, especially not after punching out the last person who'd attempted a surprise birthday party. I just put it down as his surreptitious fear of growing old.

"Close your eyes," I commanded him, turning around with a slice of my grandmother's famous chocolate cake on a plate.

He did.

I dipped my index finger in the icing and traced it along Carlo's bottom lip. His tongue slowly slid out to taste it.

"What do you think?" I asked breathlessly, completely transfixed by the way his lower lip glistened, just begging to be sucked.

"I think I should have birthdays more often," he said quietly, opening his eyes. "Grazie mille, bella mia."

"You are so welcome." I turned around. "Unzip me." I could've removed my dress myself but I sure as hell wasn't going to pass up any opportunity to get him to touch me.

Carlo dragged the zip down, his fingers grazing my skin. I shrugged the dress off and it fell – with some difficulty – to my feet. Carlo pushed my hair aside and I felt his soft lips brush against my nape and I sucked in a breath. His hands settled over my belly and I placed my hands over his before he reached out for more cream. He brushed my hair away and ran a finger down my neck before licking the cream off.

"Still taste as good?" I asked him, and he spun me around.

"Better. Dio mio, Danielle – I've been thinking about you the entire day," he fiercely pronounced, reaching behind me and unsnapping the clasp of my bra, "especially these bambinas." He tweaked a nipple and I could've come in that instant. "It was quite frustrating to be aroused when I was on the stand for murder in a courtroom filled with people."

"That's not funny, Carlo," I said quietly, reminded of his court appearance that morning. He'd told me it wasn't anything major but murder was major, wasn't it? "I hate the things they accuse you of." I was constantly berating myself for ever being judgmental enough to condemn a man I hadn't known. Being with Carlo, even for such a short space of time, only served to make my previous assumptions the tall stories they were.

He stroked my cheek as if trying to wipe away my worry. "Certo, but if their accusations had any basis, I wouldn't have been granted bail. I would have had to surrender my passport," he explained. "But I have nothing to hide and no reason to hide, bella mia. Don't look so upset." He hoisted me onto a stool and positioned himself between my legs. "Now – where's my birthday present?"

"You were supposed to unwrap me in our bedroom tonight," I replied with a smile, wrapping my legs around his waist, "but this is one gift that just can't wait."

"I wouldn't want it to," he growled, wrenching my knickers down. He paused to pull out his gun and set it on the counter then seized my hips and drew me to him. "Unzip me," he whispered into my ear. My earlier words sounded sexier coming out his mouth.

I didn't think my fingers would be able to function; they never did whenever he allowed me to take the lead. His bulge was throbbing for attention in my hand and I began to unfasten his fly, the zip catching on the swollen head of his erection. He swore in a low voice and scooped me up, walking in the direction of the cluttered tables.

"Carlo, no." I giggled, gripping his broad shoulders. "They're far too small!"

With one sweep of his hand, he cleared a table and sent empty crockery crashing to the marble floor before setting me on the polished top.

"That was bone china!" I protested, and he almost smirked.

"I'll buy you a thousand more." Carlo placed himself between my thighs again and I wantonly spread myself for him, propping myself up on my elbows.

"All I want is you," I told him, watching as he loosened his tie before undoing the buttons of his shirt. "I think that's all I've ever wanted."

A deliberate smile spread across his face. "Silenzio, Danielle. Let me do all the talking." His shirt was open now and his chiselled, scarred chest was mine to ogle. Silently, he pulled his trousers and boxers down and, with painstaking precision, found my engorged clít with his fingers. "You're more than ready," he whispered, dipping a finger inside me. "Sì, cara. You're soaking wet for me."

I ached for him. It was a physical pain that nagged at my nerve endings, my muscles, my bloody everything.

Carlo seemed to understand that. With no further preamble, he pulled me to him and lifted my legs over his shoulders. I bit my bottom lip in anticipation when I felt his c0ck at my wet opening, hard and demanding. I was dripping with need.

"Happy birthday to me," he said in a thick voice, slowly easing himself inside me. My muscles eagerly clenched around him in a vice-grip, welcoming him, and he released a guttural groan, his fingers tightening around my legs.

He slid out and I instantly felt incredibly empty but before I could say anything, he drove himself inside me, sliding in up to the hilt and making me writhe beneath him from the fullness. The table was probably going to break but that was the least of my concern. The only thing that mattered was my orgásm. I could feel it building up inside in me as he thrust in me again and again, his erection swallowed up by the abyss that was my pússy. Every thrust, every sensation because of that thrust, was driving me insane with desire, with the need to feel fulfilled, the need to come.

"Oh, hell," I gasped when I could feel myself getting there. "Cosa fai? Don't you dare stop!"

But he wasn't, because he was just as lost in this wave of passion as I was.

"I won't," he groaned, thumbing my clít and eliciting a sharp cry from me. "Can't."

With one final plunge, he came, the force of his cum spurting inside me prompting my own backbreaking climax. I felt the table wobble beneath me but with Carlo steadying me, there was nothing to fear. Still inside me, he leaned in and kissed me, exhaling heavily. I looped my arms around his neck and parted my lips for him, his tongue exploring my mouth all over again. Before I knew it, he was leisurely rotating his hips, amazingly erect once more. I tightened my grip around his arousal once more, my pússy – among other things – still vibrating from the aftermath of his perfect assault.

His mobile vibrated when it was over and I could take no more. Muttering to himself, he dug into the pockets of his trousers and removed it, glancing at the screen.

"Danielle? What does Charlie mean?" He shoved his BlackBerry into my face.

I read the text aloud as I hopped off the table: "HBD, mate. Eleganza, 9pm. Leave the missus." I mentally groaned. Charlie, who had quickly given himself the title of Carlo's new best friend, was about as subtle as a heart attack. "I suppose you have a party to get to?" I gave Carlo a weak smile.

His eyes became slits. "Oh, you will pay, you sneaky little –"

"My tits feel a little sore," I cut in, tweaking a hardened nipple. "I love it when you suck them, caro."

As I'd expected, his eyes zoned in on that one tender bud. "I'm getting the feeling that you've cast a spell on me."

"Oh, but you love it," I told him, quivering as he palmed my breast.

"Like I said, cara, you're going to pay."

"Isn't he beautiful?" asked Carlo, transfixed by the blurry ultrasound image in his hand.

He sat on the edge of the bed with it, his fingers delicately tracing the fuzzy outline of the baby growing inside me. I had the distinct feeling that he would never let that photograph go; not for all the money in the world.

"How do you know we're having a boy?" I asked him, peering over his shoulder. "Are you psychic all of a sudden, caro?" I pushed aside his soft curls and kissed the back of his neck. He flew upwards as if he'd been shot.

"Keep doing that and I won't be able to get back to work." He gave me a wide smile. "And I'm not psychic. I merely have a...hunch."

I'd told Dr. Gordon that we didn't want to know our baby's sex. She'd agreed, then asked if we'd like to come over for supper. Unlike my easygoing brothers, I still had to get used to her permanent residence in my father's house; the house we'd all grown up in. I wasn't ready for a family dinner yet.

Carlo's eyes hooded as he watched me shrug out of my nightgown. "This was supposed to be my lunch break, Dani."

"Yes, I know."

"And while it was fascinating to go to the hospital with you," he continued, already loosening his navy-blue tie, "I do have a busy schedule."

"I know that, too." I rose to my feet and began the task of unbuttoning his shirt.

"First trimester. Cristo, Danielle, that's all I can think about," he said gruffly, stopping my hands by clasping them. "That, and you. You and Mickey." He scooped me into his arms and sat on the bed, setting me onto his lap. "Do you think I'm getting soft?"

I unbuckled his belt. "No," I replied, and stuck my hand down his trousers. "You're hard. Definitely hard."

"Dani," he groaned, "I have to go. Merda, I really have to go."

I bent forwards and kissed him. "I'm sure Dominic Marino can spare you for an hour." Fridays were strictly for meetings with his seedy-looking lawyer. I knew that, yet I also knew that for Carlo, my doctor's appointments with his stepmother-in-law were top priority; this baby was top priority.

His hand gripped the back of my head as he took over, deepening the kiss. "Fúck it. He works for me," he growled once he pulled back.

I loved impromptu afternoon sex, especially because it felt like I was permanently horny. Sex was the single thing on my mind when our bedroom door was unceremoniously shoved open.

"What the hell do you think you're doing, Theresa?" Carlo snarled in Italian, heaving me onto the bed as he flew up in a rage. I scrambled for my gown and pulled it on, tightening the sash around my waist.

"Scusi, signore," Theresa said, her voice shaky and hoarse. "Signora."

"On your knees," a voice snapped from behind her, and only once Theresa slowly crumpled into a heap were we finally able to see a wild-eyed Angelo looming over her, a gun pointed at her head. He held onto Mickey – my innocent, trusting son – with his free arm.

"Sonofabitch," Carlo cursed, "I will kill you."

"Get in line, you traitor," Angelo told him.

"Let Mickey go," I said.

"Why don't you shut up, puttana?"

Carlo sprang forward and Angelo instantly pressed the gun against Mickey's temple, simultaneously kicking Theresa forward. She squealed. I squealed. Carlo froze in his footsteps.

"You know, signore," Angelo began, jiggling Mickey on his arm, "you really should invest in real security. It's a big fúcking disgrace for a big, powerful man such as yourself to have sitting ducks as bodyguards."

"That's six murders," Carlo said quietly. "Six murders, Angelo. Are you stupid?"

"Yeah, I'm a real idiot," he retorted. "Shut the fúck up before I shoot your kid."

"Shut up," Mickey seconded, trying to grab the gun. "Shut up, Papà."

"You learn fast, kid," Angelo said to him before turning to look at us. "Now, we're going to play a little game, capisce? It's called Truth or Angie-Pops-Boy's-Brains-on-the-Persian. Catchy, no?"

It took me a few seconds to realise that I was crying and that Theresa was kneeling at my feet, sobbing loudly.

"I am so sorry," she wailed, burying her face in her hands. "He came out of nowhere. Dio mio, I'm so sorry!"

"It's not your fault," I murmured, pulling her up onto the bed with me. "It's mine. It's all my fault." Angelo was mad with me. My fault. My fault.

"I'll give you a five-minute head-start before I rip your heart out," Carlo warned Angelo, and I silently pleaded with him not to provoke his nutter of a cousin into doing the one thing that would make my world fall apart.

"No, you will sit your ass down and tell the fúcking truth for a change, Carlo Donafrio." He paused. "Sit."

"Sonofabitch," Carlo repeated, obliging Angelo and sitting on the edge of the bed. My hand instantly came around his and he squeezed.

"This first question's for me: Hey, Angie, would you happen to know who murdered that McGowan person?" He paused for effect. "What, Carlo? The name doesn't ring a bell? Matthew McGowan, owner of The Swish? Nothing?" He glanced at Mickey. "Your papà has an atrocious memory."

"I didn't kill him," Carlo replied monotonously.

"No, you didn't." Angelo glared at him. "Because I did."

Carlo instantly jumped to his feet. "And you silently stood by and let my name get dragged in the mud for a crime I didn't commit?" He swore in Italian. "When this is over… Angelo, you will die."

"Who do you think I did it for, you dumb fúck?" Angelo spat. "I did it for you! He was our competition. McGowan's empire was as far out as Milan! He was going to steal business from right under your damn –"

"So you tortured him? Beat him up until there was barely any DNA left to identify him as human? That was –"

"Oh, please. Don't pretend that you go around preaching peace and sunshine, Carlo," Angelo interjected. "Just how many lives have you taken? Remember – the truth."

"Go fúck yourself." Carlo shook his head. "Scusa, Mickey," he quickly apologised. "We shouldn't be cursing in front of my son."

"Go to hell." Angelo's gaze shifted to me. "Do you really believe your husband's lily-white image? It's all an act, I can assure you, cupcake."

"Angelo, please," I said softly. "He's just a child. Please. Give him to me."

"Maybe if Carlo answers my goddamn questions…" He twirled the revolver around to emphasise his point.

"What do you want?" Carlo snarled.

"How many, Carlo? How many men have you killed just for looking at you funny? And Danielle? You might wanna take notes, signorina. We might be here for a while."

I rubbed away the tears and simply concentrated on my son's face. He certainly didn't look like a boy with a gun pressed against his bare thigh. No, Mickey looked like he was enjoying this unprecedented meeting.

"Venti," Carlo said, more to himself than to anyone else, as if saying that he'd taken twenty lives in Italian and in hushed tones would make it any better. "But that was in another lifetime, Dani," he continued, finally looking at me. "I'm not proud of who I was as a kid and I will spend a lifetime trying to atone for losing control...but I am nothing like this sick fúck."

"You're hurting my feelings, cuz. Still, you're right – we're nothing alike because you're worse." He waved the gun about, gesturing at the room. "All of this? It's a dollhouse. Who are you kidding, Carlo? You can't be a family man. You can't be anything but a Donafrio."

"I used to think the same thing," Carlo countered, balling his hands into fists as he rose. "So what do you want? A place in my will? Money? My silence? Cristo, Angie – that is my son you're pointing a gun at! Your nephew!"

"Your son? Don't you mean the product of a session of jerking off?" Angelo scoffed. His face clouded over. "You wrote me out of your will for him?" He shot a dark look at Mickey, who was blissfully mumbling to himself as he toyed with the front of Angelo's T-shirt. "After everything I've done for you, Carlo? This is how you repay me? Humiliating me so that I can't show my damn face in public?"

"Your beef is with me and only me. Why don't you let everyone else go?"

"You must think I'm an idiot," Angelo retorted. "There're six bodies out there with my bullets inside them. I've got nothing to lose. I'm going away for life. Might as well go with a bang." He paused, a sly look on his face. "You want your kid so badly? Catch."

And he launched a gurgling Mickey into the air.

I went for him.

Theresa went for him.

Carlo was faster.

Angelo pulled the trigger.

Epilogue

"Mummy, ask me again. Ask me again."

"Okay, okay," I said, feeling slightly frazzled as I pulled the cake out of the oven. I set it on the marble counter before turning to look down at Mickey. "Capital of...Madagascar? Take your time with this one."

He closed his eyes for a few seconds before opening them again and announcing proudly, "Anta..." He paused. "Antana...I don't know how to pronounce it yet, but you know what I mean, right, Mummy?"

"Antananarivo," I said slowly. "Yes, pet. Mummy always knows what you mean." I ruffled his unruly mop of coal-black curls. "Why don't you go upstairs and change?"

He wrinkled his nose. Mickey hated anyone messing with his beloved hair. "Okay." He scampered out the kitchen and left me to clean up while waiting for the cake to cool before putting it on a platter and icing it.

The candles came next – eight, big blue ones that stood proudly in the centre of the chocolate cake. I opened the big tube of Smarties and elaborately placed them around the candles before standing back to admire my handiwork. I still got a tad bit sentimental every birthday.

And who can blame me? I thought. After all, I nearly lost him once.

I shook my head. Today wasn't going to be one of my nightmarish reminiscing days. Today was going to be filled with joy and irritating family members and plenty of cake and booze.

"Looks good enough to devour right now," Jules' voice came from behind me, cutting short my mental pep talk.

I smiled and turned around. "You were supposed to get here earlier."

"I know, I know," she said, squeezing herself into a chair at the table. "I woke up late and Charlie...well, you know how Charlie is. Time is a figment of the imagination with him." She dipped a finger in the icing bowl and brought it to her mouth. "Where's the birthday boy, anyway?"

"Upstairs. Miraculously, I didn't have to fight him out of that dreadful Ben 10 costume."

"Hey, my husband bought that with love." She grimaced.

"What is it? Is everything OK?" I asked anxiously.

Jules nodded quickly. "Everything's fine. Your nephew's going to be the next David Beckham, is all."

I laughed, reaching down and placing my hand over her ever-expanding belly. "God forbid." As if he'd heard me, Charlie Jr. kicked in agreement. "And where is my tardy brother?"

"Oh, he's outside with Adam, setting up the jumping castle," Jules said, forgoing her fingers and grabbing the spatula out of my hands. She promptly scraped up the remainder of the cream.

"I have no idea who's going to get on it, seeing as how Mickey specifically said that he doesn't want any other children over." I shook my head with the memory of that particular conversation. "Really, Jay. He came up to me the other day and informed me that he wants family only. What sort of eight-year-old doesn't want other screaming eight-year-olds at his birthday party?"

"Mickey Donafrio?" Jules offered in response. "The boy's a genius, Dani, and geniuses are bizarre. Remember when he could barely say two words? Now what? He's memorising the Bible, the Encyclopaedia Britannica and the telly guide. I could barely read the fúcking cereal box when I was eight!"

"His teacher keeps saying we might have to enrol him into one of those special academies for gifted children. Would that be too much too soon?"

Jules shrugged unhelpfully. "I don't know, babe. I'm only having my first baby. You should discuss it with –"

"Signora?" A voice interrupted her.

My eyes swivelled to the doorway. "Yes, Theresa?"

"Your parents are here and Alessandra broke Signore Adam's iPhone."

I sighed. "Oh, Allie. Third one this year," I muttered to myself. "Jules, living room. Can you waddle there?"

"Very funny," she replied dryly, pulling herself to her feet. "I'll have you know that I could just pop right now, but that won't stop me from kicking your arse if you so much as say the w-word again."

"Good to know," I said, laughing as I led her to the living room.

"Dani, there you are," was my mother's greeting. She folded her arms across her chest. "Your father bought Mickey a laptop. A laptop."

"He doesn't have to use it now," my father protested, giving me a slightly affected look. "Fiona got him a toy. Mickey doesn't even play with toys."

"Oh, right, but I suppose he'll reprogram the computer software and hack into the Scotland Yard?"

If I still lived in my old house, I'd have pulled my hair out in five seconds flat with the sort of bickering that seemed to be a given whenever my two sets of parents got together under my roof. Fortunately, there were about twelve other rooms I could retreat to if their behaviour persisted.

"Fiona," Jazz said soothingly, "I think that's enough." She shot me an apologetic look. "Hello, Danielle. Jules."

"Hi," we replied in unison.

"And Michael, I'm sure Mickey will appreciate anything his grandparents get for him, don't you think?" said Elizabeth, lightly brushing my father's arm.

"And where's my naughty little girl?" I asked, and Theresa scooped the writhing girl out of her hiding place under the coffee table and handed her to me. "You're getting far too heavy to carry, Allie sweetheart," I said, balancing her on my hip. She stuck her tongue out at me, a horrible habit she'd picked up from Jules. "Where's Uncle Adam's mobile, baby?" I asked her.

"I don't know," she replied, but the cheeky look on her face told me that she most certainly did.

Adam himself appeared in the doorway, a Coke in hand. "Jumping castle's up, no thanks to Charlie."

"Adam, why do you insist on giving her your mobile?" I asked him, shaking my head as Allie pulled the phone out the front of her dress. She handed it to me for examination. "She's cracked the screen. Another one bites the dust."

Adam reached out for it. "She looks at me with those big, chocolate-brown eyes and it's you begging for the last waffle again. I can't refuse. It's those satanic eyes."

"I never liked waffles, Adam," I told him, placing a kiss on my daughter's nose.

"Well, you used to beg for something."

"The last cookie in the jar," Mum piped up. "I suppose I shouldn't have been surprised that someone with such a sweet tooth would've opened a coffee shop."

"I want a cookie," Allie said animatedly. "Please can I have a cookie?"

"You can say that again. I'm starving," Jules said, finally plopping onto the couch and kicking her strappy sandals off. "Crap. My ankles look like a hippo's thighs."

"Fishing for compliments, are we?" Charlie said on his way in, nicking the can from Adam and downing it in one gulp. "Your ankles bring sexy back, Julesie-Woolsie."

"Aw, someone's definitely getting some tonight," Jules told him, blowing him a kiss.

"Excuse me while I puke out my entire stomach contents and entrails," Adam remarked dryly. "Oh, and by the way, Dani – Gio and Mia send their apologies. Mia's first Lamaze class is today and Gio's her partner."

I smiled, imagining domineering Mia and her sweet little brother working together on something. Mia had finally decided to go through with IVF treatment and was now in her second trimester.

"Can't believe she got Gio to go," I told Adam, before turning my attention back to the rest of my family. "Drinks are out by the pool. Theresa, be a darling and open the patio door? Thanks."

"Sì."

"Let's get your cookie, cara," I told Allie, heading out the living room. She wriggled out of my embrace until I was forced to set her on the ground. "All right, all right. No running." At four-years-old, Alessandra favoured scurrying about as a pastime. "Alessandra, stop," I called out when she completely ignored me and dashed down the passageway. "Allie! You're going to hurt yourself!" I

The front door was pushed open and Allie stopped in her tracks on her way to the kitchen.

"Are you an angel? Come ti chiami, signorina?"

Allie giggled. "Alessandra."

"What a beautiful name, cara mia. Aren't you going to give Papà a kiss hello?"

"Yes."

Carlo placed his briefcase on the ground and bent to pick her up.

"And just like that, she's well-behaved," I commented, smiling when she rained kisses on her father's face.

Carlo kicked the door closed behind him and met me halfway. "She's always well-behaved." He was putty in her little hands.

"I bet if she burnt the house down, you'd give her a cookie for a job well done."

He leaned in and briefly pressed his lips against mine before pulling away. "Are you jealous, bella mia?"

I laughed, watching him set Allie back down on the ground. She instantly darted away. "Stop being ridiculous."

Carlo's arms looped around my waist as he pulled me into him. "I missed you."

"I missed you, too," I said, pressing my nose into his chest and inhaling his scent. "I didn't think you'd make it."

"Neither did I. The turbulence was ridiculous. But I'm here now." His hand cupped my rear. "I hate business trips."

"How about we go upstairs and I show you just how much I missed you?" I asked, tapping my fingers against his chest.

His eyes darkened. "That sounds –"

"Papà!" Mickey exclaimed, appearing out of nowhere.

I pulled away from Carlo and allowed Mickey to jump into his outstretched arms.

"You are too big for this, mio figlio," Carlo chuckled. "Happy birthday."

"Mummy's big and you carry her," Mickey observed. "Thanks."

"Hey, I'm not big," I griped, rumpling his hair.

Mickey groaned. "Okay, Papà. You can put me down now."

Carlo obliged him.

"I won't ask what you brought me because I'm just happy you're here," Mickey proclaimed boldly, before turning on his heel and shoving his hands into the pockets of his jeans.

"I feel like he's the parent sometimes," Carlo remarked, shaking his head. "When did that happen, cara?"

"I don't know about that," I said, "but if you don't carry me upstairs for a quickie, I know I'm going to explode."

"Hmmm," Carlo mused aloud, running the pad of his thumb across my bruised bottom lip, "and we can't have that, can we? These tiles cost a shítload." His hand strayed across my braless chest and I felt my nipples harden. The noise from the rest of the house just seemed to fade away.

Carlo's hands could give me the most infinite pleasure; salve our children's bumps and scrapes – but they could also take a life. The reminder of that small fact was imprinted on Carlo's left shoulder. I wasn't aware that I had pressed my palm against his shoulder, over the scar I knew was under his shirt, until he squeezed my left breast and I snapped out of my trance.

"I'm sorry," I whispered, retracting my hand. "It's morbidly funny, but I was thinking – I shot your right shoulder and Angelo shot your left. I love you for surviving."

His brow furrowed, as it always did whenever his dead cousin's name came up. "The difference is that he didn't know how to shoot his way out of a cardboard box..." He angled his head to kiss me "...and you do."

"Actually, I don't want to talk about him. Ever." The recurring memory of Carlo twisting the madman's neck was enough of a reason not to.

"Certo. How long do you think we have before Alessandra wants to cut the cake?" Carlo murmured, cupping my face in his hands.

"Oh, about three minutes?" I figured, knowing that when it came to cake, our daughter never cared whose birthday it actually was.

"Then we definitely have to make those three minutes count," Carlo said huskily, and he picked me up, throwing me over his shoulder caveman-style.

This time, I didn't scream. I liked the view.

www.ingramcontent.com/pod-product-compliance
Lightning Source LLC
Chambersburg PA
CBHW060801210726
48292CB00013B/1628